TRICKLING SANDS

By Jerrod Fasan

Table of Contents

Chapter 1
Time Well Spent

"Come on, one more, just one more," Richard said. "After this, I'm done. You know I handle my drinks well. Besides, it would only be my second glass."

Trevor, Richard's best friend, lightly grumbled. "Okay, I guess I can stay for one more. Then, I must get home to the family. It's been a long day." Trevor slowly took a sip of his frothy drink as he stared into the distance where he surveyed the room.

With hands in a boxing position, Richard lightheartedly threw jabs towards Trevor's legs. "Come on, big guy, why do you have to stand over me all bent up? You're tall enough as it is. I can barely see your face from here." He began to pat his hand on the stool next to him. "Take a seat; life is too short to be in a rush. Come on, sit down and enjoy the moment, will ya?"

Leaning against the bar, Trevor grumbled once more. *He does have a point.* "But on a serious note, Richard, we are leaving soon, and we both drove here. Be mindful of this, please." Trevor pressed his lips together as he shook his head. "You're my friend, and I don't want something happening to you, that I could have prevented."

"Treeevor! Trevor, cut it out. No need to worry about me. I'll be just fine, bud. Now you, on the other hand..."

Trevor's eyebrows furrowed in disapproval in anticipation of his next antics. "Hey. Hey, I know where you're going with this. That was one time, and the pie on the table did look like a pillow. I needed somewhere to rest my head." Trevor's face perspired with embarrassment.

Richard slapped the table as tears treaded down his face, accompanied by bouts of cackling. "Yeah, I need to have a drink or two of what you had *that* day."

"Okay, that's it! Nic-" Trevor lifted his arm to flag the bartender down for the check as he could no longer tolerate the teasing.

Richard reached up to grab Trevor's hand. "Ok! Ok! That's it, no more. No more, I promise." His head jolted to the left as he turned to Nicholas the bartender, continuing his guffaw. "Never mind, Nicholas!" he shouted across.

Nearby patrons didn't seem to mind the escapade. The dimly lit surroundings and T.V. broadcasting sports highlights at an appropriate volume seized most of their attention. The rest were completely lost in their plumes of cigar smoke and strong drinks, immersed in their own world.

Richard continued to hold Trevor's arm suspended in the air as Trevor proceeded to scold him. "I agreed to come here after a long day's work. Being a detective isn't always that easy. But can you cut this out already?"

Richard slowly lowered Trevor's hand down to the counter as Trevor continued to give him the death stare.

Richard Hines and Trevor Hartman were best friends who lived in the town of Welder Ville. They were at their usual bar after a long day of detective work, to have a few drinks, bunker down, and relax before heading home. Richard and Trevor though opposites both in characters, and of looks, made the perfect friendship combination. Though they shared two things in common, strong work ethic, and the fact that they were proud country folk.

"I seem to have grown up, but sadly, I can't say the same for you. You're thirty-eight years old and still act like a child," Trevor scolded before he averted his eyes. "Whatever man, you'll never understand."

Richard's eyes went wide as he pointed to himself, feigning shock. "Haha, you speak as if I'm years older than you; I'm older than you by only a year." He whipped the finger that was pointed at himself through the air, as he then held it in place. "By the way, *I'll* never understand? I'm sure no one will. Ha!" Richard laughed so hard he spewed the last gulp of his drink. Grabbing a napkin, he attempted to wipe the spill off his shirt. "Aw, see what you made me do? Man, this is too much." He pounded the table as he caught his breath amid the bouts of laughter. "I'm sorry Trevor, that was just too funny," he added as he wiped the last bit from the counter. The noise would soon attract the attention of Nicholas the bartender, a good friend of the two.

Nicholas threw his white rag over his shoulder. "Alright, guys, what is it? Isn't it kind of late for this? Come on."

Richard sat up straight in amusement, stuck out his chest, and inhaled deeply while grinning. "Do you really want to know? Does 'pillow pie' help?"

"Huh?" Nicholas peered at them as he wiped the counter. "Ohhh, that? Ha! Now I see." He laughed which further vexed Trevor.

"Really? I thought you said you wouldn't mention that to anyone, especially here." Trevor squinted his chestnut-hued eyes sharply before staring intensely at Richard.

"I'm sorry, but I had to! Haha!" Richard burst into uncontrollable laughter once more.

At this point, one would think others around them would have grumbled at their doltish behavior; but it seemed the liquor and smoke made them oblivious. Some chose to ignore the behavior altogether.

Taking hold of the corner of his towel, Nicholas proceeded to wipe the sweat from his brow. "Man, I needed that laugh. But we have to tone it down a bit. You guys are laughing just a bit too loudly now. People come here to relax after a long day. We don't want to anger the drunk people who most likely had a crappy day. Drunk and angry is not the best of combinations."

Folding his lips, Richard took a deep breath. He decided it was best to change the subject out of respect for others who came to enjoy their stay. "Okay, I'm done. I promise. For now, at least." Richard placed his right hand on Trevor's shoulder once more. "Good?"

Annoyed, Trevor continued to stare at Richard. "Get your hands off of me." Normally, Trevor wouldn't mind Richard's antics so much; but he felt Richard had taken it too far by letting people in on such an embarrassing moment that he wished to forever erase from time. Or maybe it was the stack of paperwork he had to fill out all day, either way, Trevor just wasn't in the mood tonight.

"Will do," said Richard flashing a grin as he slowly removed his hand.

Trevor nodded in appreciation before dusting his shoulder.

"So, how's the wife and kid? Wasn't she supposed to be visiting her mother soon?"

"They're well." Richard sighed. "Mark will be turning seven soon and Serene is doing great. She just got back from visiting her mother a few days ago actually. She needed it. How are Tiana and the kids?"

"They're great." A few drops of beer traveled down his chin, as he sipped his drink. "Dale is getting bigger, and the two girls are growing up a little too fast. Always asking for the newest phones and such, but I can't complain. At least not until they tell me they have boyfriends. Then I'll be in trouble."

Trevor downed the reaming bits of his drink. He looked around only to see a few patrons remaining among empty wooden seats and tables.

"Great to hear, man. We have to get together again soon for a cookout. It's been a few months since last time," Richard suggested.

"Definitely. I'll speak with my wife about it and see when works best for us," Trevor agreed.

"I'll do the same," answered Richard before perking up. "Oh, and by the way, I will tell my wife not to bring the potato salad with raisins in it anymore."

Trevor covered his face as he gave a slight chuckle. "No, she can bring it. I will just have my wife make some as well, that way, people can just choose whatever they want."

Having a cookout consisting of people with different backgrounds, of course certain foods at times won't resonate as much with some. As to not disregard one or the other, it was decided that each person would prepare a dish, and from there, people can decide what they want to eat.

"Haha, ok then, sounds like a plan," said Richard.

"I think it's time we call it quits for tonight and head home. I'm sure my wife is worried, as always," exclaimed Trevor as he gave a much need stretch.

"Shows you have a good wife that loves you, appreciate that."

"Yea, I most definitely do. She surely is a blessing."

"Welp, I say let's get going," added Richard as he grabbed his jacket. "Hey Nicholas, see you later! Trevor and I are heading out."

"Okay you guys, take it easy," said Nicholas as he prepared to close for the night.

Richard exited the smoke-filled atmosphere of the bar where he enjoyed the cool crisp night air before making his way to his vehicle. As he sat, he decided to give his wife a call. But he realized he couldn't since recent events required him to disconnect the phone temporarily. Then there was the fact that he left his cellphone at work. To fill the void of not hearing her voice, he imagined how the conversation would have likely gone.

"Hey babe, I just wanted to let you know I'm on my way home. Is everything okay?"

"Yes, sweetie. Mark and I just had dinner. I'm about to give him a shower before bed. I left some food out for you for when you get home."

"Thanks, but I think I'll hop right into bed when I get back. I'm kind of beat. I just need some sleep. Of course, that is, after I get my special good-night kiss from you."

"Oh, stop it." She would be blushing on the other side of the phone.

"I'll be there soon. I'm on my way now."

"Okay."

After a long, relaxing and quiet ride, Richard finally arrived home. When he entered the house, he was exhausted. Tossing his bag on the floor and throwing his jacket on the coffee table, he was now ready to settle in the confines of his bed.

"Honey! I'm home!" he said playfully.

"There you are," answered Serene his wife, as she smiled. "I'm so glad you're home. Mark and I just finished eating dinner; I left some out for you if you're hungry."

"Come here, sweetheart." Richard, feeling confident, motioned for Serene to come closer. Upon the gesture, she sauntered over to him for a kiss. Richard took the time to relish her aroma, which was comparable to that of exotic flowers. As her lips moved away from his, he looked forward to the moment they would meet again. The two seemed as if inseparable.

Richard gazed into Serene's eyes. "I'll skip dinner tonight; all I want to do right now is march upstairs and get some sleep. Where is Mark? Is he asleep?"

"He fell asleep about thirty minutes ago. He's knocked out. He was up all-night watching cartoons. I should've turned them off sooner, but I thought it wouldn't hurt to let him stay past his bedtime once in a while. I love him so much. He'll grow up to be handsome, just like his papa," she said playfully.

"Oh, don't jinx the poor boy like that. Now, I will be just like my son and head to bed. Are you coming too?"

"I just have a few more dishes to wash. I'll be up in a moment."

"Okay."

Richard headed upstairs to shower after a long day of work; but not before stopping in his son's bedroom and kissing him on the forehead as he slept.

After a satisfying shower, there was no better way to finish it off than with a comfy warm bed.

Once in bed, vague memories flashed to the surface. Thoughts of the myriads of gruesome crime scenes he'd seen during his years in the unit came to mind; finding runaways, apprehending heartless criminals, and worst of all, dead bodies. Which is one thing most detectives hope to never see.

Somebody's got to do it. Who better than me?

He flipped one way in the bed, and then the other as he tried to find a comfortable position.

I do this for my wife and child. I can only imagine what the future holds.

Chapter 2
Peculiar Is an Understatement

Morning came and it was time for Richard to once again, prepare for work. Upon waking, Richard could not describe the feeling as nothing other than strange. Nothing felt right. He just couldn't quite put his finger on it. Even after he had a nice long stretch, he just could not shake the feeling off. Richard entered the bathroom and perceived that everything looked odd.

Man, maybe I should have skipped a drink or two last night. I don't know; I don't feel drunk. I didn't come home drunk. Maybe I can hopefully shake this feeling off soon.

Everything appeared vaguely different to Richard that morning, from the sunlight to the color of the walls. Something was off. The aura and sensations of everyday things affected him differently. The air that would normally circulate on and around his body seemed to permeate, hitting his very inner being. The sun's light entering the room seemed intensified; its glow almost seemed alive. His every footstep felt as if he was being carried by an escalator. Time itself seemed altered.

Maybe I need to eat. Speaking of which, where is breakfast? And where is Mark? Richard went downstairs.

"Serene!.. Serene! Where are you?" He didn't bother to look in the bed since it was normal for her to wake before him.

Richard walked to a nearby chair within the room and collapsed into it. Taking a brief but intent moment to study and survey his surroundings. Wondering the cause behind him feeling strange and the subtle, but noticeable difference in his environment. "Gotta get back up," he said to himself, lightly groaning as he hoisted himself from the chair.

Since the day they got married, Serene always had Richard's breakfast and orange juice waiting for him when he woke. The smell was like a second alarm clock for him. That morning though, Richard didn't smell the aroma of his morning meal. Combined with the fact that he was already feeling strange, he instantly became worried. What was worse, he didn't see his beloved son Mark. Confused and worried, Richard went back upstairs to search for his wife and son.

"Serene? Serene?" shouted Richard, running his hands through his dark brown hair.

"Yes, Richard, I'm in the bathroom," Serene called.

Serene was an effortlessly beautiful woman, age thirty-four. She was gentle, nurturing, and calm; it seemed like nothing ever could annoy her. Her skin resembled ivory, with hues of peach, in its full maturity.

"Where is Mark? Aren't you supposed to be getting him ready for school?"

"I know, I know. It's just —I can't quite put my finger on it. I just feel...strange. It's not a sickly feeling, just an odd one. It took so much effort just to turn the faucet on, and I mean a lot of effort. It was almost as if I passed right through the knob," said Serene as her ocean blue eyes gazed into the bathroom mirror.

Hearing this, Richard felt even more uneasy.

"It's strange you say that; I feel the exact same way. It looks like I'm going to be late for work. I overslept by almost an hour. My real concern is Mark. Where is he?"

Serene raised her eyebrows as she rubbed her eye wearily. "I don't know; maybe he's still asleep."

Mark was Serene and Richard's only child. A bright young kid, and despite only being six years of age, Mark knew to avoid dangerous situations at all costs. He knew the dangers of walking off with strangers or leaving the house alone. Knowing he had the comprehension of such things, Mark's parents had great reason to be worried.

Richard and Serene desperately searched their three-story home for Mark. But after quite some time, they came up empty.

"Oh God, this can't be good." Richard rubbed his head anxiously. "Mark! Mark!"

They searched their home from top to bottom; yet, there was still no sign of him anywhere.

"This isn't good. We've checked everywhere. I think it's time we called the police."

Richard went into the living room to grab his coat and realized he left his cell phone at work. The wall trembled as he punched it in frustration. *Dammit...what now?*

Richard was very protective, of his wife and son; and due to previous events, Richard was forced to disconnect the landline phone service due to receiving phone calls from strangers. A few were the usual scam calls that everyone receives on occasion. But one day, Serene got a call from someone who claimed they knew her; while at the same time refusing identify themselves. Despite her numerous pleads for the individual to identify themselves, they refused to. As a result, Richard felt it was best to take this precautionary measure for the time being until he could get to the bottom of it.

Furious, his fist landed upon the wall once more. *This is all my fault...*This couldn't have come at a worse time. Richard and his wife lived in a gated community where many of their neighbors also work in law enforcement. Even though law enforcement doesn't pay exceptionally well, Richard was able to move his family there due to his father leaving him a good amount of money when he passed away. Despite the comfort and security, he still chose to be extremely careful.

By this point, they had already checked every part of the home, including Mark's room. Still, there was no sign of Mark anywhere, and their concern only escalated.

He cursed under his breath as he clasped his hands behind his head. "I forgot my phone at work and we can't even use our landline due to those imbeciles calling our home damn near every other night... dammit! Mark could be in trouble and hurt somewhere. How can I be so careless…"

"No, don't say or think things like that. I'm sure Mark is okay." Serene placed a hand on Richard's face, trying to calm him despite being worried herself. "Think positive; we will find him."

* * *

Down at the Welder Ville police station, Richard's colleagues were becoming concerned as well. Though no one was more concerned than his best friend Trevor. For Richard to be late, let alone not show up at all, was extremely unusual.

"Hines has never been late, not once in all these years," said Corporal Maribel. "I don't care that he's late, but he could've called to let us know that he would be. This is what's most worrying to me."

"Yeah, I know." Leaning against the desk, Trevor Hartman crossed his arms. "This isn't like him."

"Coffee anyone?" Officer Chanel asked. "Let's stay calm. I'm sure everything's fine. Maybe he had something to do concerning his family. We should be hearing from him soon, I'm sure."

Hartman smiled at the offer. "I'll take some coffee; thank you."

"Hartman, don't you and Hines usually hang out after work for drinks?"

"Yeah, last night, we had a drink or two, but I'm sure he wasn't drunk when we left the bar. I made sure of that. He was able to drive home. If I was worried, I would have dropped him off myself. This is all to strange."

"How about someone just give his cell phone a call?" Chanel suggested.

"Good idea," responded Hartman. "I'll give him a call right now."

Despite his continuous efforts, no one picked up the phone. At this point, everyone in the office started to worry.

"Come on, come on...pick up, Richard." Trevor's leg bounced nervously under his desk as he anxiously awaited a response. Having gotten any response, he gathered his colleagues to give them the bad news. "I tried to call again and again, but there was no answer. I checked my office phone log to see if he tried to reach us. I even tried to call their landline and still, nothing. How about you guys?"

Officer Chanel shook her head. "Unfortunately, nothing on my end as well. How about looking in his office? Maybe he left his phone there."

"Good idea."

* * *

Back at Richard's house, he and Serene continued their search for Mark.

"His book bag, his coat, his boots, everything is still here," Richard said. "He couldn't have left the house. It's freezing outside, so he wouldn't have wandered off on his own. Dammit! All I had was one duty as a father and that was to be a protector, and I failed!"

"No, Richard. This isn't your fault. We don't know what's happened. Don't think the worst. We have to believe Mark is all right."

Serene's words of reassurance calmed Richard's nerves a bit, though he was still flustered.

"Maybe you're right, but we've checked everywhere I can think of. Where else can we look? I have to go out and look for him."

* * *

Mark was in a dark and cold place, shaken and scared as he called out for his mom and dad.

"Mom...Dad..."

Mark had covered himself with a large dusty sheet in an attempt to find comfort in a place of darkness and solitude.

"Mom...Dad...I'm scared," Mark continued to utter his breath.

As Mark hid behind the large dusty sheet, he could hear rattling, banging and what sounded like running water. Shivering, his heartbeat with terror. Mark should have gotten up and ran, but as he was paralyzed with fear, he found it impossible to do so. He heard faint voices around him, and at one point, he could have sworn he heard his name being called.

"Mom...Dad...," he whispered to himself as he remained all alone.

* * *

Richard nervously fidgeted his hands as he put on a brave face. "I'm going outside to look for Mark. Maybe a neighbor down the street will let me use their phone to call for help from the station."

Serene's delicate hands reached out to Richard. "Do you want to at least put your coat on?"

"Being cold is the least of my worries," Richard remarked with a little more attitude than he intended. Gently, he held her by the fingertips. "Sorry..."

"It's ok Richard..."

Rushing towards the door, Richard made his way to the exit in search of Mark; but oddly, when he tried to leave, the door would not open.

"What the...what in the world? What's up with this door!"

"Maybe it's the cold outside. We just had a snowstorm a few days ago, so maybe some of the ice has lodged itself in between the door."

"No, that can't be it. Yesterday, I came in and out without any problems. Damn! What is going on? First, I wake up feeling like crap and now Mark is gone. What could I have done to deserve any of this? I do my best help everyone out and this is the karma I get in return, just great."

Serene took a deep breath. "I'll look around the house a little more while you try to get the door open."

Clenching his jaw, Richard stormed to the opposite side of the house. *Maybe the back door will open.* The knob twisted and turned; but as with the front door, it showed no sign of opening. Enraged, he lowered his shoulder and readied it before charging. "Open dammit, open!" His chest heaved in and out as his nose flared. Walking backward, he continued to stare down the door. He charged once more. "Ahhhhh!" he shouted before throwing his shoulder against the door. Yet as with before, Nothing. The door merely produced a slight bang, but showed no signs of opening.

* * *

The detective unit was still on edge about Richard not showing up or calling the unit. It had been nearly two hours. The department knew they had to do something and fast.

Trevor nervously played with his chin hairs. "I just checked Richard's office and it turns out he left his cell phone here." Trevor sighed as he held Richard's phone. "Weird. Richard always makes sure to carry his phone with him; I can't remember the last time I called, and he didn't have it with him. He always kept his phone with him, always."

"Maybe I can go out to his residence to check upon him. I'll let you guys know if I find anything," Chanel offered.

A thud ensued as Trevor placed down his coffee. "No, Chanel, you stay. I'll go. I'm more familiar with Richard's family. You showing up unexpectedly at their door may make them uneasy."

"Okay Trevor. If anything, reach out."

As Trevor drove out to Richard's residence, he wondered what could have happened and hoped he didn't discover the worst-case scenario. An uneasy feeling began to develop in his stomach; he tried to imagine the best, but that uneasiness would just not go away. Trevor changed the radio station to positive tunes to help his mood, but that also did little to help. He finally settled on turning the radio off, as the sound of nothingness was enough for him.

Richard...Richard, please be okay. Just last night we were out having a good time. I don't know what's happened, but I'll find out soon. I'm sure you're okay.

* * *

In the darkness, little Mark remained paralyzed by terror. Huddled under the dusty sheet, he continued to hear banging and rattling once more. At that moment, Mark's fight or flight response wanted to kick in, but his fear was fighting against it.

"Mom! Dad!" said Mark, sobbing. He continued to hear faint voices all around him in this state of darkness. It was getting colder, and the darkness showed no sign of retreating.

Chapter 3
No One Else Was Fit for It

As Trevor got closer to Richard's residence, a mixture of emotions settled in. Maybe he'll discover that Richard was safe and sound. Or…Trevor refused to consider the "or." Trevor's been a detective for years now and had encountered the worst of the worst; he was almost immune to it. Though as he'll soon find out, he could never in a million years fully prepare himself, for what he was about to discover.

Upon reaching Richard's home, he stuck his head out the driver window to get a better look. *I see his car parked upfront, so that's a good sign. Richard, Richard, why must you always worry me so much?* Trevor grinned thinking about his old friend's antics.

"Man, I knew I shouldn't have let Richard have that extra drink. He wasn't wasted when we left the bar. I guess it kicked in when he got home. I'm totally going to get him back for that 'pillow pie' joke he always brings up," he said to himself. *Yea, once I walk in there and discover you passed out drunk, I'm never going to let you live it down.*

Trevor parked and approached the front door. His nose widened as he took a deep breath to ease some of the anxiety. "Okay, here it goes," he said before knocking. Placing his ear to the door, he continued to knock, awaiting a response.

He couldn't hear anything from the other side of the door. Stopping to survey his surroundings, he only noticed a female passerby walking her golden retriever.

In the air his hand went as he proceeded to knock once more. *Come on, answer. Answer Richard, please.* At the door he stood for quite some time, waiting for an answer, but to his dismay, it didn't come. *Ok, maybe they are all just still asleep, y-yea, that's it, they are still asleep.* Despite his attempts to imagine the best outcome, he could not help but to imagine the possibility that something bad could have happened.

Trevor, remembering that they always hid a spare key knelt and lifted the doormat. "Got it!" he said as he held up the spare keys in triumph.

In the midst of the uncertainty, he attempted to make light of the situation. "Sorry to do this guys. I really hope I don't see anything too embarrassing, that I may never be able to un-see." Trevor turned the key a couple of times before finally getting the door open, where he then stuck his head inside. "Richard!.. Serene!" He called out as he awaited a response. *Man, where are they?* He thought as he put both hands to his mouth in an attempt to amplify his calls. "Richard!.. Serene!" he called out once more. "Richard! are you there! Richard!"

Trevor called his friend's name for another minute or two before deciding it was time to go in.

Anxious, he began to fidget with his trench coat as he walked deeper into the home. "Richard!"

Taking his time, he began to walk around the house as he took note of his surroundings. A few things stuck out as peculiar. Random objects were scattered about as he heard running water from multiple sources.

"Richard! Serene! Anyone here? Man, where are these guys? This is not good. I better call the department and let them in on what I've seen so far." Reaching into his brown trench coat, Trevor retrieved his cell phone. "Hey, Chanel? Hi, yes. I'm at Richard's, upon arriving, I noticed that his car is parked in front. So I know for sure he got here safely after last night. I rang the doorbell for some time, and no one came to the door, so I found a spare key and let myself in. I see no signs of anyone, not Richard, his wife, or his son. I'll continue to look around and update you guys periodically."

"Roger that Major," Officer Chanel responded. "If you find anything that you need assistance with, do not hesitate to reach out to us."

He rubbed his temples with his unoccupied hand in an attempt to ward off stress. "Got it, thanks."

* * *

Richard and his wife Serene were in the basement, looking for Mark when they heard something, that caught their attention.

Richard held one finger out towards Serene. "Shhhh, honey, do you hear that? I think someone is upstairs, listen."

Both Serene and Richard stretched their necks towards the basement stairs with open ears.

Afraid, Serene cupped her mouth as she stared into Richard's eyes. "Honey, I hear it!" she whispered.

Gritting his teeth, Richard continued to peer up the basement stairs. "I'll go check it out. Maybe it's Mark, at least I hope it is." *If it is an intruder, with my very hands will I break him.*

As Richard left the basement in a hurry to see who, or what was in their home, Trevor was making his way into the living room closet.

Richard quietly began to walk up the basement stairs. With dilated eyes, he peered around the door. "Where is he..." Quietly he walked into the living room, his jaw clenching with every passing second. *Come out so I can see you, you scumbag.* To his surprise, there was no one there. Ensuring the intruder was nowhere hiding, he made his way up to the second floor.

Exiting the living room closet, Trevor's gut instinct told him to check the basement.

Across his forehead the back of his hand went as he broke out in a nervous sweat. "Richard! Serene! Mark! Are you down there?" Suddenly, he heard what sounded like a voice. "Mark?"

Quickly, Trevor stormed down the basement stairs. Hyperventilating, he nearly tripped and fell on the last stair. *What the hell is Mark doing down here by himself.*

In a state of confusion, Serene turned and smiled towards Trevor. "Trevor, thank goodness you're here. This whole day has been so strange." She paused as she noticed Mark peeking out from under a sheet. "Oh, Mark, thank goodness! Why didn't you come out when we called sweetheart? I had no idea you were there; we were looking all over for you!" When Mark didn't respond, Serene turned toward Trevor. "Trevor, why isn't he answering?"

To her surprise, Trevor also completely ignored her as he tried to find the light switch.

"Let me help you," she said as she got to her feet.

She reached out to grab the switch, but no matter how much she tried, she could not get a hold of it. Fortunately, Trevor managed to turn it on.

Trevor looked around frantically. "Mark! Mark!" he called out. He continued to look about until he saw a small figure huddled in the corner of the basement with what seemed to be a dusty old sheet.

Mark was still completely immobilized by fear, only peeking out once earlier when he heard Trevor's footsteps coming down the stairs. He could hear a chain swinging nearby; the fear proving overwhelming. With each passing second, he did his best to fight the fear; but the more he fought it, the more it only seemed to increase. Suddenly, Mark would let out a scream loud enough to send a shock wave through anyone in the area.

Serene knelt before her son, shocked, as she covered her mouth. "Mark? What's gotten into you?"

Trevor pulled the blanket from Mark before wrapping his arm around him. "Mark! Mark! I'm here, it's okay, it's okay," he said as he hugged him in a warm embrace. "What happened? Where are your mom and dad?"

As all of this was happening, Serene was reassuring Mark that everything would be okay. Serene nervously fidgeted her hands as they shut and close. "My son! My son! Oh God..." Her blues eye stared at Mark as the tears flowed. "Mark, my baby, everything will be okay. Wait here for mommy." After reassuring her son with words of kindness and comfort, she rushed upstairs to let Richard know that Trevor was in the basement with Mark.

Her long hair flowed as she looked nervously about. "Richard! Trevor is downstairs with Mark in the basement!" She called out.

"I'm coming!"

Relieved, Richard followed Serene to the basement. *We checked the basement over a hundred times and didn't see Mark. And Trevor? But how? Why is he here? He must have been worried that I didn't reach out to the department or show up at work today.*

In the basement, Trevor was talking to Mark, trying to find out what exactly was happening.

Trevor placed both hands on Mark's shoulders as his voice trembled. "Mark! I need you to talk to me. Where are your mom and dad? I need you to tell me!" Trevor closed his eyes as he took a deep breath in an attempt to recompose himself.

Mark continuously shook his head, clearly anxious. "Upstairs." His amber eyes looked at Trevor in a state of anxiety.

From the look he saw in Mark's eyes, Trevor knew whatever the outcome was, it wouldn't be good.

"Okay, Mark, you stay right here, you hear me?"

"Okay."

Trevor stormed up the basement stairs; and as he was rushing through the house, Richard, and Serene crossed path with him.

"Trevor! Trevor! What's going on?" screamed Serene and Richard loudly. But their cries fell on deaf ears.

Trevor reached the top of the stairs where he headed to the bathroom. Confusion ensued as he looked about. "Why is the bathroom water running? And why would they just leave it and keep it running? This isn't looking too good." With great haste, he hurried into Richard and Serene's bedroom.

"Richard! Serene!" Trevor called out, turning his head in every direction.

As he approached their bed, a sense of dread and doom suddenly overtook him. Trevor saw a large, thick blanket over the bed. As he walked towards it, it felt as if time itself slowed down. The seconds it took to reach the bed and pull back the sheets, felt like an eternity. Trevor noticed a handgun wedged between the large wrinkles of the blanket. Not just any handgun, but Richard's service arm. Trevor's heart stopped for what seemed a moment as he laid eyes on the 40 caliber. Lifting the sheets, Trevor would find the lifeless bodies of Richard and Serene. His body froze as chills ran up and down his frame; tears instantly filling his eyes as he tried to register what he was beheld before him. Trembling, his hands shook violently amid the dreadful sight. It was as if all life had left his legs, yet, somehow, someway, he remained standing. Mournfully, he stared at his best friend and his wife's lifeless bodies.

Richard and Serene remained confused as to why was Trevor, was completely ignoring them.

Richard threw his hands in the air, his sandy complexion turning red with anger. "What the hell? I tell you; this day cannot get any stranger. My best friend is in my home without me knowing and now, he completely ignores my presence," he said before placing his heads upon his waist. "Serene, you go in the basement and keep an eye on Mark, while I go see what's going on."

Serene made her way back to the basement to comfort her son.

"Oh, Mark, we have been looking all over for you," said Serene as she rushed towards him in an attempt to embrace him. In the process of doing so, her arms and body went entirely through him; what's worse, he didn't reach out in return to hug her back. "What in the...wha—wha—what is going on!" cried Serene. She stumbled backward; looking down at her body as she wailed. "Mark! Mark! Talk to me! What is happening!"

Richard had finally reached the second story. Looking on, he saw that Trevor's back was turned towards him while looking over their bed. Furious, he stormed towards him. *You're going to have a lot of explaining to do buddy*. "Trevor! Hey! Hey! I don't know what your problem is, but you have crossed the line!"

As Richard reached out to grab Trevor's arm, something caught his attention. Narrowly looking upon the scene, he would notice a hand was dangling from the bed, causing him to second guess his eyes. Richard slowly pulled his hand away from Trevor and moved toward the unsettling sight. As he continued to approach, he would periodically look back and forth between Trevor and sight with great bewilderment. Then, he saw it—his lifeless body lying next to that, of his very own wife.

Chills instantaneously radiated throughout his frame. "What in God's name." He glanced up at his best friend's face, only to see tears flowing profusely. "Trevor…" he uttered before averting his gaze back to his and his wife's corpses.

Stumbling, Trevor collapsed into a nearby chair. Next to Richard's body was that of his wife's Serene, as she lay lifeless in a pool of blood, under the thick blue blanket.

"Sereene! Sereene!" Richard almost forgot that lying next to her lifeless body was that of his own. He reached out to embrace her and in doing so his arms entirely went through her motionless body.

Serene heard Richard's intense wailing, wailing she had never heard in all her years of marriage with him. She rushed upstairs to discover the cause of his lamenting, running as fast as she could. A mix of emotions soon filled the home, emotions consisting of fear and unease.

Her delicate face perspired as she stood with a trembling frame. "Richard! What's going on?" She asked as she entered the room. She could see that Richard was kneeling before the two bodies in their bed. As she continued to wonder, her eyes peered towards them. She slowly walked to the bed as her mind tried to rationally make sense of the irrational. "What in the world; who are those people in our bed?" She asked as she walked towards it. Glancing over, she noticed Trevor sitting with a blank expression upon his face. "Richard, Trevor, tell me what is happening!"

The gravity of the situation finally set in as her eyes widened then relaxed in a state of shock. Her chest heaved up and down as her mouth tremored as she fought to get the words out. Her fingers outstretched toward her deceased body. "Is... is that me? Richard? What is going on? Please! Tell me what's going on!"

Hearing Serene's voice again after what felt like an eternity, Richard immediately stood up and embraced her. He wailed uncontrollably, his eyes reddened with grief. "Oh God, I don't know, I don't know."

Serene shook her head; refusing to believe what was taking place. "Richard... th—those are our bodies. We, we are...dead?" A calm breeze flowed through the window as she stood in silence, her arms hanging at her sides while Richard continued to embrace her.

Richard continued to hug Serene without uttering a word, relishing the fact that he was holding her in his arms once more. For the next two hours, Serene and Richard consoled each other in complete silence, accepting that they were no longer alive.

Trevor sat motionless, the tears pouring from his eyes revealing the sorrow of his heart. The police department tried on numerous occasions to reach him, but it seemed his mental made him oblivious to everything around him, including the many phone calls that came his way.

Chapter 4

It Takes a Village

Back at the department, the team became increasingly worried about Trevor as it had been a couple of hours since he last reached out to them.

Officer Chanel approached Maribel. "I tried calling several times; he hasn't answered. What should we do?"

"Give it a little more time," Corporal Maribel answered. "If he doesn't respond in a few minutes, I'll send a team out to check on him."

* * *

Just as Richard and Serene came to grips with the fact that they were no longer alive, Trevor slowly but surely, began to accept the same. Trevor began to become somewhat aware of his surroundings and noticed someone was contacting his walkie. With the strength that remained in his body, he picked up and answered the call.

His weary eyes closed as he answered. "M—m—major here."

Leaping out of her chair, Chanel answered. "Major? Oh, I am so glad to hear from you. Is everything OK? We have tried so many times to get in touch with you."

"R—r—roger."

"Everything okay there? Why do you sound distressed? Talk to me Trevor."

He forced an inhale as he tried to break the terrible news. "We have a double homicide. Richard and his wife...they are dead."

"W-what? Richard is what?" Chanel asked before pausing as she regained her bearing.

"H-he's…he's dead."

In what seemed like an instant, tears burst forth from her eyes. "Send a team out to Trevor's location! Immediately! Now!" She shouted before stumbling against a table for support. Richard was a friend, brother, to the many who knew him.

It wouldn't be long before most of the unit got word.

Corporal Maribel fought to restrain her tears amid the dreadful news. *Calm down Maribel, calm down. You must stay strong, they need you. Stay strong Maribel, stay strong.* Adjusting her suit, Maribel stood as she bit her lip. "It—it—" She took a deep breath and shut her eyes tightly as she prepared to address the unit. "We must remain strong and composed. This is deeply saddening news, but as we all know, Richard would not want this to get us down." Though she didn't show it, she was as equally heartbroken as the others.

Soon, everyone in the facility would get the disheartening news and as expected, the atmosphere became that of significant dejection.

Officer Timothy lamented. "Richard? Richard?... no way. Please tell me this is a joke. No way... but how? Why?" Officer Timothy had been with the unit a little over two years now and in those two years, he had grown a great attachment to every member in the unit. But no one in the unit had impacted him the way Richard had for when he came in a nervous wreck, Richard's bubbly personality made it feel like home.

Closing her eyes, Corporal Maribel shook her head in disbelief at what she was about to say. "Homicide, double homicide. His wife was also a victim."

"Oh god," said another under their breath.

Balling his fist, Officer Timothy punched the nearest wall to him. "I-I tell you; I'm going to kill whoever did this! I promise!"

Officer Maribel sternly gawked at the young officer. "Hey! Hey! Timothy, don't you say those words again. You hear me? We already lost two people here; we don't need to lose another."

Officer Timothy heeded her words as he clenched his fists in an attempt to keep his anger at bay.

Caressing her eyes, Chanel wiped away her tears. "Should we call Sheriff Asher and let him in on the news?"

"No, that won't be necessary," Corporal Maribel said. "He's on his way now. To give him news like this while he's driving could be potentially dangerous. I doubt he'll be able to think straight. Asher should be here soon. We'll let him know when he arrives."

"I can't believe Richard is gone…Richard, he's really gone…"

* * *

Meanwhile, back at Richard's house, Mark was in his room huddled underneath his blanket. Trevor snapped out of his deep trance once more at the sound of Mark's sobs. Stumbling out of his chair with as much strength as he could muster, he got up and went to tend to him.

Gently, Trevor placed both hands on Mark's shoulders. "Mark, you have to talk to me, okay? What happened today in this house? You have to tell me."

"I...it was..." Mark uttered before breaking out in tears. Trevor decided not to press him anymore about the situation, at least for the moment.

"It's okay; it's okay. How about you go outside and sit on the patio. You shouldn't be up here right now."

Mark wiped his tears as he nodded.

As Trevor walked with Mark, he kept his arm around his shoulders to make sure he didn't look back in the direction of his parent's bedroom.

Trevor made his way to the living room and walked around somberly. On the fire-mantle, he saw a picture of Richard and him from when they first started at the department eight years prior. He held the frame to his face as tears began to pour once more. *Richard, why?... why?* Leaning against the fireplace, wearily, he rested his head against his forearm. Recovering some strength, he took the time to look at pictures of Richard and his family hanging about the wall. Trevor realized he would never be able to look his best friend in the eyes again, to hear his voice and most of all, to experience his carefree spirit. Pictures were the closest he would ever be to experiencing that moment once again; and coming to this realization. it tore him within. He continued looking at all the pictures he could find of Richard and his family until backup arrived. *Why him, of all people? This man didn't deserve any of this...*

* * *

Sheriff Asher pulled up to the station completely unaware of Richard's death. He exited his vehicle and entered the station, expecting the cheery "good mornings" he was usually greeted with. That day, however, he would only be greeted with tears and mourning.

Immediately upon entering, he noticed that everyone in the room was tense. "Guys, what happened?"

Many were crying while some wore looks of genuine despair and regret. Everyone appeared as if they didn't want to be the one to break the terrible news to him. But they all knew, sooner or later, he would have to hear about it.

Clutching his belongings tightly, Asher clenched his jaw to where the tendons showed through. "Tell me what's going on! That's an order!"

Corporal Maribel's shoes clicked as she walked towards Asher. "It's Richard. He has... passed away." Asher remained silent at the disturbing news as he refused to believe it. Therefore, Maribel took the time to continue. "He didn't call or show up to work today, therefore, Trevor went to his house to find out why. That's when Trevor called into the unit to tell us the terrible news. Not only was he discovered dead, but his wife also. It appears to be a double homicide. Trevor informed us that it doesn't appear to be a murder-suicide."

Maribel spoke to everyone about the situation as she would in any other investigation, with straight facts, putting her emotions aside. But Maribel knew this would hit Sheriff Asher the hardest; he was almost like a second father to Richard. Asher was close friends with Richard's dad, who introduced Richard to him as a young teen. Richard's father always felt that Richard would make a good sheriff one day; but now, he would never get a chance to reach that rank.

Finally, Asher understood the ramifications of what he was just told. His cup of coffee slipped from his fingers where the warm brown liquid splashed all over. Somberly, he shook his head as he refused to believe what he was told. "Richard...no, not Richard, no."

The majority of the team came over to console him, knowing this was truly devastating news to him.

Maribel gently grasped his forearm, her touch calming and reassuring as she sought to provide him with a measure of comfort during this difficult moment. "Sheriff, come, take a seat."

Maribel's age was reflective of her wisdom, a mature woman, age fifty- one to be exact. Despite her age, she remained sharp and witty. She treated every person who was younger than her in the unit as if they were her own children. Though she was loving and gentle, when the need arose, she could be as stern as anyone. Her brunette hair was typically kept in a bun as she sported her sliver-lined eyeglasses, which she peered through with ocean blue eyes.

Everyone sat in silence except for the occasional sobs. No one was sure as to what to say.

Asher mustered all his years of wisdom and experience possible to contain his deepest emotions. He, like Maribel, knew he had to set a positive example for everyone.

Asher exhaled as he prepared to stand. "Richard was like a son to me." Biring his lip, he attempted to hold back the grief. "I took him under my wing as a young man. Many years ago, I would always tell his father that he would grow up to be such a great man and he became that and more. He grew up exceeding my expectations. Everyone, please, leave the office for a bit. Just give me some time to think, thank you."

Chanel approached Maribel. "Corporal, would it be alright if I went out and checked on Trevor? I am sure he could use one of us right now."

With brief, but deep consideration, she agreed. "Sure, I guess that's fine," she replied, her voice carrying an undertone of caution. Just be careful...please."

Grasping both of Maribel's hands, Chanel looked her in the eyes. "I will." Any pretense the officers usually made to be brave, and stoic was thrown out of the window. Richard's death revealed the softer side in all the officers.

* * *

Another department in a nearby county was alerted to the crime and sent a few detectives to investigate. While Trevor stood in the living room, he would soon hear sirens blaring in the front, as they made their arrival. Before stepping out to meet his comrades, he would give a picture of Richard and his family one last look. Placing a hand on the frame, he proceeded to bow his head. "I'll figure out who did this to you. I promise."

Just then, Sheriff Daniel entered the home. Calming approaching as he sympathized, he placed a hand upon his shoulder. "It's okay, soldier..." Stepping back, he took the moment to look Trevor in the eyes. "Your unit informed me and my men of all the details before we arrived. I just want to say that I'm sorry to you and the unit for the loss. This not only affects you guys, but us and the town as a whole. We truly lost a great guy," he said before taking a moment. "I think you have seen enough here today; you should sit and wait in one of the vehicles. My officers and your backup will take it from here. Thank you, Major."

He managed to smile in appreciation. "Y—y—yes, thank you," he said as he walked away, broken-spirited. Trevor made his way into the cold air, which nearly deprived him of the little energy he had remaining.

Officer Bailey from the other unit took notice of his disheveled state. "Whoa, whoa man, take it easy, I got you." Bailey and a few of his colleagues helped to escort Trevor to the vehicle.

"You stay here and take it easy. I'll stay with you just in case you need anything. Sheriff Daniel and a few others will investigate. I know there is a young kid here by the name of Mark. We were instructed to have him sit inside a vehicle until someone can escort him to a nearby hospital. You know, just to make sure he is fine physically and mentally. Do you know where he is?"

Wearily, he gestured with his head. "On the patio...I instructed him to wait there until backup arrived."

Bailey placed a hand on Trevor's shoulder for reassurance. "Thanks, sit tight. I will inform the others so they can escort him."

Inside the home, a forensic team along with Sheriff Daniel and other detectives analyzed the crime scene. Despite being a seasoned detective, Daniel's heart constantly sunk at the sight of the unfortunate scene. *I've always heard only positive things spoken about Richard. A man of great character and leadership. The monster, the soulless being who did this, I will make sure they rot in jail.*

The forensic investigator kneeled in the crime scene area. "After a brief analysis, it appears this is definitely not a homicide-suicide case. The positioning of the bodies points to a homicide, but strangely, the bullet entered and exited at an odd angle. It appears a bullet struck Richard in the heart, killing him almost instantly. That same bullet traveled through him, striking his wife in the kidney and hitting her abdominal aorta. She more than likely had massive internal bleeding. Due to the positioning of her body, she wasn't killed instantly."

"Poor guys. Thanks for your analysis," replied Sheriff Daniel.

Officer Chanel arrived at the scene. With great enthusiasm, she rushed out of the car to meet Trevor. Reading and willing to give him her unwavering support.

She approached the nearest officer. "Officer Chanel here, and you're?"

"Officer Maven," he said before extending a hand.

"Pleasure to meet you. Do you know where Trevor is currently?"

"Oh sure, he is right there in the squad car. Orders were given for him to stay there until the investigation concludes or until someone is able to escort him back to his unit."

"Thank you." Chanel quickly set her sights on Trevor and made her way over.

As she approached, she noticed that he was staring out the car window and into the sky. There was no sign of emotion on his face. He appeared exhausted and in his own world.

Upon meeting him, Trevor was instantly met with a warm hug. "Trevor, are you okay?" It took a while for him to even register that someone was talking to and embracing him.

"Wait, what? oh, hey Chanel. I'm glad to see you. How is everyone holding up at the station?" He sighed, staring into the distance as the reality of the situation seared his conscience once more.

"We're holding up," answered Chanel as worry was written over her face. "We were concerned about you. Come on, how about I drive you back to the department? One of the other officers will drive your vehicle back to the unit for you."

"I appreciate it. I'm going to say bye to Sheriff Daniel before we head out." Trevor needed to know what happened. The men from the other unit had only been there twenty minutes or so, but they had to have had more information than he had at the moment.

"Take your time."

As Sheriff Daniel was stepping out of the house and away from the crime scene, Trevor was already meeting him halfway.

"Hey there, Major."

In humility, Trevor looked away as he tried to find the proper words. "I just wanted to thank you for the words of encouragement, it meant a lot. I'm sure our officers could have handled this, but I'm glad you guys could step in to help."

"Major, I have been in this field for nearly fifty years. Working in the field this long, you unfortunately become immune to what would make the average human break down. Don't thank me, this is my job. On the other hand, I can't imagine how you feel. You and Richard were so close and let me tell you, Richard would have been proud of the way you carried yourself. If anyone had to choose who to look up to between me and you in this situation, I surely hope they choose you. Now head back to the squad car, I am sure some of your colleagues are waiting for you."

"Thanks, Sheriff. That means a lot coming from you." He paused a moment, not wanting to seem too eager. "Have you guys found anything?"

"By the way Trevor, I hope you're not thinking about doing anything irrational. I know he was one of our own, but we have to solve this the legal way. Get vengeance the proper way." He paused as if contemplating whether he should tell Trevor what they know. Squinting, he averted his gaze to gather his words. "This was not by any means a murder-suicide. Someone killed these two. One bullet was fired and it first entered Richard's heart, killing him. According to the forensic team, his death was instant, and he didn't suffer a painful end. Unfortunately, that same bullet exited his heart and entered his wife's kidney, leading to her death. For some reason, someone wanted Richard dead. It doesn't appear they intended to kill Serene. She was simply collateral damage. What's worse, they used Richard's very own gun against him. I just don't see why anyone would have anything against such a man."

"Well, were there any signs of forced entry? Any stolen items?"

"So far, absolutely no sign of forced entry anywhere. There were a few items that seemed moved about, but their house wasn't ransacked. This is a strange case, but fingerprints should lead us to the murderer quickly. I do hate to say this but, in an event like this, everyone is a suspect, even six-year-old Mark."

"Mark? Why would you even suggest it was him? He loved his mom and dad and would never in a million years hurt them." Trevor tried to contain his anger. "Besides, you said Richard's own gun was used against him. Richard told me he always stored it up in his bedroom closet in a locked box that requires a key to open. For those reasons, I say it's impossible for Mark to be responsible for this crime. He has no idea where Richard kept his gun, and even if he knew, he would have never been able to reach it," explained Trevor.

"That's good information. I'll look into it." Sheriff Daniel turned to Lazario, one of the forensic technicians. "Lazario, I need you to go into his bedroom closet and search for a box."

"I'm on it."

As the forensic scientist carefully searched the closet, Trevor and Sheriff Daniel trailed behind him and watched from a distance.

"It appears from here that everything in the closet is neat and untouched," Sheriff Daniel said.

After searching for some time, Lazario found the box. Holding the box, he began to turn it in every direction. "I see that the box is unlocked, and upon opening it, it appears there is nothing inside."

"I guess this is the box that Richard spoke to me about; this is where he usually kept his firearm. Do you think the murderer got to the box somehow, unlocked it, and used the firearm against Richard?" asked Trevor.

The box twist and turned as Lazario continued to inspect it. "From my years of experience doing this, I can tell you here and now, a murderer didn't get hold of this box. It would not make sense for the murderer to find the box, take the gun out, lock the box, and then take his time to place it back in the closet, and neatly at that may I add."

Trevor sighed deeply. "None of this makes any sense. I just..."

"Major, you've seen more than enough today. I need you to meet Officer Chanel at the squad car so she can escort you back to base," said Sheriff Daniel.

Trevor realized that he was back in the room where his best friend and his wife's bodies lay, which were now covered with a white blanket. He mustered every bit of strength in him to hold back his emotions. Trevor pressed lips together. "You're right. I think it is time I left."

Trevor went back to the squad car where Chanel sat waiting for him. Meanwhile, Mark was sitting in the back of an ambulance, awaiting transportation to a nearby hospital for a quick initial inspection. Trevor stared towards Mark before approaching Chanel.

"You know what, on second thought, you go on without me. I'll ride with Mark to the hospital, so he isn't alone."

"Major, I think it's best you come with me back to base. You do not look fit for this right now, and Sheriff Daniel has a great unit. I'm sure they will take good care of Mark. Some of our men are here also."

"No, I have to go with him Chanel. Mark just lost his mother and father. Now it's my responsibility to make sure Mark is safe. I can't let Richard down by doing otherwise."

Chanel thought for a moment before deciding this may have been best for Trevor, especially since Trevor and Richard were the best of friends. "Okay, I guess it's not a problem, but please, all I ask is that you be careful."

"I will. See you guys at the station soon."

The unit came to Trevor's aid just like a well-oiled machine. Such cooperation would surely be needed going forward; for this, was only the beginning.

Chapter 5

A Moment of Reassurance

Back at base, everything was quiet. The shock that Richard left them so soon, so suddenly, and in such a tragic way called for nothing other than grief and reflection.

Officer Berth, a rookie at the station pianoed his fingers along the desk as he sat anxiously. "I hope the rest of the unit and Hartman arrive soon. I really want to know the update concerning Hartman. He must be devastated after witnessing his best friend in such a state."

"I know, but Trevor was the best person to go out to the residence in this situation. He was very close to Richard and knew him and his family best, so no one is to blame here," assured Corporal Maribel.

Corporal Maribel glanced back to see Sheriff Asher sitting in his office as his face rested in the palms of hands. She felt he had spent enough time alone, and now it would be best if he were outside with the rest of the unit.

Maribel held up a finger. "Hold on guys, I will be right back."

"Sheriff, how are you?" She asked upon entering.

"Who would do this to them? And why? He never had any issues with anyone and everyone in Welder Ville knew him as a good guy. No one deserves such a fate, especially Richard and his wife. I have dealt with many homicide cases in my career, hundreds in fact, but none have ever hit me this hard before. "

Maribel understanding the ramifications, struggled on the best response. Especially dealing with the gravity of the loss and how it touched Asher. Eventually, her years of experience came through. "I applaud you for staying strong for the unit. I know this is hard for you. We will catch whoever did this, that I can assure you of. Trevor and Chanel should be arriving soon, and they should be able to update us more on the situation."

This comforted Asher a little, but then his thoughts shifted to Richard's son. "Poor Mark. The kid must be going through pure agony right now. Only God knows what he heard and saw, during all of this."

"No, I am sure he is receiving the best attention possible at the moment. From what I understand, Trevor is not sure if Mark actually saw his parents' bodies. I hope he didn't, for the sake of his sanity," said Maribel caringly before placing a hand upon his shoulder. "Come, sit outside with us, everyone needs your strength and wisdom at the moment." Maribel tried to gently prod Asher, knowing that there was still work to be done.

Sheriff Asher entered the main space where he gave the team words of encouragement. The unit still felt the blow of the news, but Asher's talk extinguished much of the grief and agony they were feeling. Asher wrapped up his talk with additional words of reassurance.

Taking the time to look each and every person in the eye, Asher began to pan the room. "So, for these reasons, we must remain strong. Richard would not want us to remain in a state of defeat and despair, he would want us to pick ourselves up and keep pushing. He wouldn't tolerate us getting too emotional. This is not to say he would not want us to display these inherently human emotions, but rather, he would not have wanted us to dwell on them. Preferably, he would want us to conquer them before they conquer us. With that, let our mourning be passionate but brief, for life must go on." His words of encouragement emboldened everyone, certainly, his speech was of much help.

As Sheriff Asher wrapped up his talk, Officer Chanel arrived at the station.

Excitedly, officer Timothy jumped out of his chair as he stared towards the window. "Chanel! Trevor! They're back! Everyone, they're here!" Everyone faced the main entrance, poised and ready to envelop Trevor in words of love and reassurance. This was certainly a day of firsts. The station hadn't experienced a situation as unique as this before, so it called for sensitivity they often discarded before going to work. As opposed to hiding their emotions and maintaining a level of professionalism, today, they would need to tap into their sensitive sides.

As Chanel drove up to the station, she could feel everyone's gaze on her and her vehicle. Her colleagues all watched as she exited the squad car, but they quickly noticed someone was missing.

Timothy couldn't help to blurt out what everyone was thinking. "Where's Trevor?"

Removing her hat, she nervously averted her gaze. "Yes, I know. The initial order was to make sure Trevor returned back to the unit, but Trevor insisted on doing what he felt was best. He decided to go with Mark, Richard's son, to the hospital."

A forceful exhale escaped from Maribel's nose as she became irate. "Trevor is where? I gave you an order to safely bring Trevor back to base. If you knew he was being stubborn, you should have buzzed me or Asher to let us know what was happening. We would have been able to talk him out of it. His mind must be all over the place right now and you know this, Chane... You know this."

"But I—"

Asher interjected. "No need to explain yourself Chanel. You did the right thing by letting him go. If anything, being with Mark is probably Trevor's best remedy right now. Trevor not only always spoke highly of Richard, but also of Richard's son. Go unpack and relax, Chanel, you have said enough." Asher sternly looked to Maribel to ensure she agreed with his sentiments.

Sheriff Asher was the elder within the unit, age sixty and regardless of his age, he had not lost his stride. The strands of gray hair mingled with black only gave credence to his wisdom. He exhibited it well, as he slicked it back in a fashionable, yet mature style.

* * *

Trevor was riding in the ambulance with Mark to Shed's Town hospital, which was located not too far from Welder Ville. The ambulance was warm and comfortable compared to the cold, harsh winter elements outside— an atmosphere that induced sleepiness. Mark had beaten Trevor to it as he was already passed out in a deep slumber, the rest much needed. The ride was smooth, no bumps in the road or cars blaring their horns. It felt to Trevor as if the ambulance was all alone on the road in a moment of peace and solitude. Trevor leaned forward on the bench, then back, repeating this process a few times in the hopes that he could keep himself awake until the ambulance arrived at its destination.

Trevor's phone rang; but to his surprise, he didn't recognize the number. Upon closer inspection, he would notice the area code was from the next town over.

Groggy, he held the phone to his ear. "Hello?"

"Yeah, hi Trevor. It's Sheriff Daniel. I know we just saw each other and that you're still processing everything, but I wanted to let you know about an encounter I just had."

Trevor was exhausted and still processing, but if the sheriff had any information pertaining to the case, he needed to know. There was no time to waste.

Wearily, Trevor rubbed his eyes. "Hello, sheriff. Go ahead; I'm listening."

"Well, while we were analyzing the crime scene, one of the neighbors to the right of Richard's house, came over. They thought it would be helpful for us to know that Richard had a rather heated argument a couple of months back with the neighbor to the left of his house.

Trevor sat up straight as the news struck his interest. "What was the argument about?"

"That's the thing. The neighbor wasn't sure. They just saw them exchanging words across the fence. Ben Warren, the neighbor was waving his fist in the air a lot. The neighbor thought it would be helpful for us to look into it."

"Did you go question Ben?"

"He wasn't home when I tried the door. Since your station is closer to the area, I figured I would let you know in case you wanted to look into it and try to question him another day."

"Thanks, Sheriff Daniel. We will stay on top of it."

Upon hanging up, Trevor felt hopeful that the case would be closer to being solved. He needed to know who killed his best friend.

Exhaustion set in.

Trevor leaned back against the wall, utilizing the moment to relax and rest. He closed his weary eyes to get whatever rest he could out of the ride, and it would be soon before he fell into a relaxing slumber.

* * *

Trevor entered a dream state where he found himself sitting on the front porch of his home; the sun was out but not too overbearing. The breeze resonating through the neighborhood could be described as nothing other than blissful. He seemed to be the only one outside. No cars, no people, just him and nature. *What a beautiful day. If only every day could be like this. What more can you ask for if you have your health and life itself, life in all its glory, such as it is now. Man... if only people could appreciate all of life, everything it has to offer. Not many people realize life itself also includes those who are dear to you. No one knows what it is like to lose a piece of that precious life until it's gone. Your memory consoles you to try and help you cope, but it only helps so much.*

As Trevor relished the moment, he noticed that someone was walking towards him. But the sun shined too brightly for him to make out the face. What he could see at that moment was that the stranger was wearing all white clothing as if the sun itself, was taking notice and attaching itself to him. The man walked closer and closer to Trevor. To his surprise, it was Richard. The dream was so lifelike that he rejoiced to see Richard once more, even believing, he had come back from the dead.

Trevor's eyes widened in disbelief. "Richard? It's you! Richard!"

With a welcoming smile, Richard sat next to Trevor. "Nice to see you again friend. I know you're deeply moved that I am gone."

Trevor quickly interjected. "What do you mean you're gone? You're right in front of me talking. You're here Richard, you're here and I'm happy to see you again. Everyone has missed you; it's been years since you have been gone. I remember when you first left us, everyone was heartbroken; I always thought of you and prayed to see you again. I thank God my prayers have been answered." In the dream, it appeared to Trevor that years have passed since Richard's death when in reality, it had only been hours.

"Trevor, I won't be returning with you. I've visited you to assure you that I am okay and that I want you to move on with your life. Your wife and family need you. I am fine, and now you must make sure the same goes for you and your family. I do have one request for you. Please watch over my son. I am less worried about him when he is with you. Even as you're now in the ambulance with him, I see the care you show towards him. Mark has always looked up to you and I am sure he will continue to."

Trevor's eyes began to water. "What do you mean you aren't coming back with me? What ambulance?" Trevor asked confused, refusing to accept the words of his dear friend.

"What you see now is not what you will see when you awaken. I have only come to visit you Trevor. I know the visit may seem soon, but it is never too soon to pay a dear friend a visit. It is time I go now."

Trevor's eyes continued to fill with tears. "But where is Serene? Is she back too?"

"Again Trevor, I am not back, at least in the way you used to see me. As for Serene, she is doing well, just as I am. The rest and peace we have now, no one in their wildest dreams could imagine having on earth. You're a great man, a man of great character, a righteous man. One day I know we will see each other again. As for now, you have a life to live, so don't waste it in mourning. Instead, turn that mourning into strength and continue to do the outstanding work you have been doing. I must go now Trevor. Farewell."

Trevor was gradually pulled back into a vacuum of white light as Richard slowly faded away in the distance until Trevor could no longer see him. He was soon back to the reality of knowing that his dear friend, was no longer with him.

Chapter 6

Piecing Together the Shattered Mirror

Trevor awoke as the ambulance was pulling up to the hospital's entrance. Trevor wiped a tear from his eye as he stood down at the ambulance's floor. "Richard..."The ambulance jerked slightly as the paramedics pulled to a stop. "We are here. We will help escort you two inside," said one of the paramedics.

"Here, put this around you," said Trevor to Mark, putting his jacket over his shoulders as they prepared to exit the vehicle into the cold winter air. "Mark, it will be okay. We're here just to make sure you're fine. The doctors will check you for any injuries, and you may be asked some questions along the way. Don't feel overwhelmed by them, take your time to answer. If they ask you to say what you saw or heard last night, please Mark, let them know. The only way we can better help you and this situation is with answers and honesty."

Mark stared at Trevor as he nodded.

Trevor and Mark were escorted inside where they were immediately tended to by Doctor Walsh.

Walsh knelt on one knee before Mark. "Doctor Walsh here, nice to meet you gentlemen," he said before focusing his attention on Mark. "Young man, what is your name?"

With eyes of dejection, he looked the doctor in the eyes. "Mark," he replied.

"Hi, Mark. I am Dr. Walsh," He said before standing up right and shaking Trevor's hand. "What is your name? And how are you related to this young man?"

"Trevor, Major Trevor. He is the son of a close friend of mine who recently passed. I decided to come along with him to make sure he is all right and to at least have someone he knows around him." Trevor asked the doctor to speak with him for a brief moment in the corner of the room. "He lost both his father and mother-just today. Unfortunately, they were found dead from an apparent homicide."

The doctor paused, clearly shocked. Although he had seen and heard news like this for many years, he had yet to get accustomed to hearing it, whenever it involved a child.

"Thanks for elaborating. I will do a quick physical, just to check for any bruises; but from here, he looks fine. When I am done, I will have the psychiatrist do an analysis, just a few brief questions. They will be simple in nature."

The doctor performed a brief but thorough exam, ensuring Mark was free of any physical harm. "Just as I guessed, he is cleared to go. You can go to the desk and speak with a receptionist, and they will let you know where to proceed next."

Trevor and Mark were told to go to the third floor to meet the psychiatrist.

"Hello, young man! And may I ask, what is your name?" the psychiatrist inquired with a playful tone that was both inviting, and warm. His voice carried a lightheartedness that immediately put the young Mark at ease.

Despite this comfort, Mark found it hard to look the psychiatrist in the eyes. "Mark," he answered as he kept his gaze averted.

The psychiatrist was informed ahead of time of the gruesome details, of the situation. Therefore, he prepared himself on how to greet, as well as answer them. "Nice to meet you, Mark. And you sir, what is your name?"

"Trevor, Major Trevor."

So far, everything was running smoothly during Mark's trip to the hospital; everyone seemed polite, prompt, and most of all, considerate.

"Mr. Trevor, you may take a seat right there," he gestured as he prepared to talk with Mark. "Mark, I want to ask you a few simple questions, okay?"

"Okay."

"Mark, how are you feeling as of now?"

It took a few seconds for a response. "Sad..." he answered somberly as his voice trailed off.

"Okay, what are your thoughts at the moment? Do you want to be left alone? Do you feel you need a friend?"

The tears which flowed revealed the unfortunate state of his heart. "I want my mom and dad."

Seeing Mark's depressed state when answering the question brought forth the tears, Trevor had been fighting back. The psychiatrist took a deep breath before asking his next question. He too fought his emotions as he attempted to maintain a calm, and professional approach. "What makes you feel sad?"

Before Mark could answer, Trevor interjected. "What do you mean, what makes him feel sad? Do you not know what just happened? I'm sure there are certain things you can ask in situations such as this, but that doesn't need to be one of them. Are you here to help him? Or make things worse?" Asked Trevor calmly, but sternly. Trevor's exhaustion from the day was clearly affecting him, making him overly protective of Mark.

The doctor pulled Trevor aside. "Look, children at this age are very vulnerable mentally. The sooner we can help him express his emotions, the better. Keeping emotions bottled up for too long can be harmful to a child's mental state. He just suffered a traumatic experience, and he may be looking for someone to talk to, and it is best done in a professional environment. The questions posed today will be brief and short; as he continues to come, then we will gradually go more in-depth. Some children take a very long time to overcome grief, especially of this magnitude. I assure you this is for the betterment of Mark."

Trevor took a long, deep breath, before agreeing with the psychiatrist in hopes of avoiding a back-and-forth argument, creating a hostile environment for Mark. Trevor understood that this was the psychiatrist's job and knew he had done this on many occasions, so he placed his trust in the doctor's hands.

Closing his eyes, Trevor sighed as he accepted his proposition. "Fine."

The doctor finished up his questioning without any further disruptions. "Mark, I have one last question. What will make you happy right now? How about a treat?"

Mark nodded.

"Perfect, here you go buddy. It's an apple-flavored lollipop, my favorite as a kid. Mark, you sit right here and enjoy it while I speak with Trevor for a moment. Here you go, sit tight buddy."

Mark took the lollipop where he held it somberly in his hands. His head hung towards the ground as he sat on the edge of the chair, showing no intentions of unwrapping the candy. The psychiatrist took notice of it.

Trevor was instructed to come to a corner of the room where the psychiatrist briefly discussed the session and future visits.

"This visit was generally done to engage not only his responses, but for me to also analyze his body language. Luckily, he didn't display any severe emotional distress or bodily anxiety. Sometimes, this can be a good thing, while at times, it can be a bad thing. When a child displays severe emotional distress early, that is just his or her way of venting out the stress. When done with the guidance of professionals, it can altogether be eradicated. On the other hand, when a child displays little emotion, it can mean he is bottling it up, which can be extremely negative. So, over the course of our future sessions, I will take note of his progress."

Trevor smiled as he reached out his hand. "Thank you, sir and again, I apologize for being aggressive earlier. I just want the best for Mark at a time like this, but I realize you're a professional and I should respect you as such. I will certainly let you know during future sessions, how he is behaving in general. I know all the information provided will be of help."

"That would be perfect. I will let you two get going. Do you know who his new caretaker will be?"

"His aunt Laurel, the sister of Mark's mother has volunteered to take custody of Mark. I know for sure she is a great match because I know how close she is with Mark; she loves him as if he is her own." Richard and Serene sadly never got to writing a will, but Trevor was sure they would want to have Mark in her care. Aunt Laurel was so much like Serene in appearance and disposition, which was nurturing and tender.

"Perfect. Those are all the questions I have for today; you two are free to go now."

* * *

A few days after the tragic incident and after pressing continually to have custody of Mark, Aunt Laurel was finally able to pick him up. Aunt Laurel was a kind woman, just like Mark's mom, and to no one's surprise, she also bared a striking resemblance to her. Laurel could never have children of her own due to health problems. Now that she had Mark to take care of, she would treat Mark as if he were her very own. Aunt Laurel hoped she and Mark would find solace in each other, solace they could never obtain otherwise in this situation.

Trevor visited Mark and Laurel to see how Mark was adapting to his new life. Trevor was expecting the best for Mark as he was living in a very large home that was furnished, updated, and in a neighborhood that fortunately, had plenty of children around his age. Trevor rang the doorbell, eager to see how well Mark was coping.

After a few moments, Laurel came to the door where she greeted Trevor with a warm welcome. "Oh! It's you, Trevor! So happy to see you! Here, come in, make yourself comfortable. I was just cooking up some dinner— pasta with meat sauce. There is plenty for all of us. Mark is just upstairs; I will go and tell him he has a special visitor."

Aunt Laurel was a woman in her early thirties, alluring in appearance as in persona. She loved to wear house gowns that displayed warm colors to reflect the tones of her home. Her amber colored hair complimented her attire, which she liked to wear free flowing.

As Trevor waited patiently for Mark, he could not help but notice how nicely put together the home was. The vibe was relaxing and positive, and anyone who stepped foot into the home would feel as if they belonged. Her home exhibited warm colors of amber and orange and the scent was of sweet cinnamon, almost reminiscent of freshly made apple pie. After a few moments of taking in the serenity, Laurel and Mark came downstairs. To no one's surprise, Mark was excited to see his friend Trevor.

Trevor opened his arms as Mark rushed towards him. "Mark! Hey pal, how are you feeling?"

"Good."

Trevor noticed that Mark's words had become shortened; he was not the jubilant child he once was, who spoke all his thoughts. Instead of the animated conversations filled with joy and spontaneous thoughts, Trevor now encountered a more withdrawn version of Mark.

"Just what I wanted to hear. Are you being good and treating Aunt Laurel nicely?"

Mark smiled as he nodded.

Trevor smiled sympathetically, reminding himself to keep high spirits in such trying times. "If you continue to be such a good boy, you and I can go out later this week for some ice cream. How does that sound?" Trevor asked.

Mark seemed interested in the offer but only replied with, "good."

A bit put off by Mark's behavior, Trevor sighed as he kept his smile. "Great... so continue to be the good boy you are, and the ice cream is all yours. How about you head upstairs and continue with what you were doing while Aunt Laurel and I have a talk."

Trevor was trying his hardest to get to the bottom of who murdered Richard and Serene. So far, the station had been unable to contact Ben Warren, Richard's neighbor. They called his work but found out he was in Spain. When asked the reason, his coworkers only knew that it was sudden. He called out of work the night before leaving and said he didn't know when he would be back. Considering how cryptic Ben's jaunt out of the country was, he was the prime suspect so far in the investigation.

But Laurel and Serene had a brother-in-law named Haden, who happened to be married to Richard's sister Bertha. Unfortunately, Haden had an alcohol problem and, in many instances, verbally abused Bertha. Sometimes he even physically assaulted her in states of rage. The unpredictability of his outbursts turned what should have been a safe haven for Bertha into a battleground, where love and respect were overshadowed by anger and hostility. Bertha, being Richard's sister, called for Richard's intervention on occasions, which at times would become ugly. Trevor was aware of Haden due to the fact that Richard had spoken of him many of times and never in a good light. In Trevor's mind, he was a major suspect in the crime, even number one on his list.

"I am so sorry you have to see your sister depart at such a young age. If I could reverse time and be there to stop it, God knows I would. The forensic team said she didn't appear to be the intended target, but that in no way gives the murderer any leeway with me."

Aunt Laurel sighed as her sister once again came to mind. "Yes, indeed, this has been weighing down on my soul heavily. I think about her nearly every minute of the day. To be honest, the only thing that is helping me keep my sanity is Mark. When I see Mark, I see Serene. I hope I can be a mother to Mark as my sister was, though, in reality, no one will be able to replace her. She was more than a big sister to me; she was a role model. When our parents passed, she helped me through the grieving process. You could even say she was not only like a sister to me, but also a mother. I will look after Mark with all my being, the same way my sister would have looked out for me if I needed her." She paused to reign in her emotions. "You may be wondering why I am not crying bitterly. It's because when I think of Mark, all of that sorrow fades away. I think of all the good things I would do for him. Not only because I love him, but because he is my sister's son. Sorrow no longer has a place in me when I consider the things I will do for Mark. I feel proud knowing I will help raise Mark to become the man my sister would have wanted him to become. She has already instilled much wisdom into Mark that I am sure will not depart from him, even in old age. Serene will always be near and dear to me in my heart."

Tightly, Trevor pressed his lips. "I am not one to express myself emotionally to others, but what you said really touched me."

"Oh, it's okay, men cry, women cry. Crying is part of the healing process, let it all out at once, rather than bit by bit."

"I guess you're right. But something has been on my mind a lot lately concerning Haden and Richard. I know they didn't get along very well. Are you aware of any recent conflicts between the two?" Laurel and Bertha had become close after Serene married into his family. They met at their wedding and hit it off so well, that they spoke on the phone weekly.

"Come to think of it, a few weeks ago Bertha told me that the two got into a heated argument. Richard's sister loves Haden despite his actions towards her. Bertha begged Richard not to have him arrested. Richard loved his sister, so he didn't pursue it any further, but at the same time, he made sure Haden got a few words. The last incident between the two was rather bad, almost to the point of coming to blows; it got pretty ugly. Bertha mentioned to me how after Richard left, Haden said that he wanted to hurt Richard. She didn't think he meant it and would never go that far with his actions; so, she never reported it to the police or told Richard."

Trevor boiled inside and came to the conclusion that Haden is certainly his number one suspect. He took a deep breath to compose himself. He decided to change the topic to Richard's funeral, which would take place in two days.

But before he could ask, Laurel spoke. "I know you said that Serene's death was an accident, but did the station ever look into the weird phone calls she was getting?"

"Weird phone calls?" This was the first time he was hearing of the phone calls. Richard had mentioned something about disconnecting his phone, but he thought it might have been just another thing he needed to fix and didn't get around to, like his security system.

Laurel continued. "Yes, she was getting phone calls from a man claiming to know her. But he wouldn't tell her who he was. She said his voice sounded familiar, but it really freaked her out. Richard disconnected the phone until he could get to the bottom of it."

"When did she start getting the phone calls? I can't believe Richard didn't catch the guy." Trevor was reeling from the new information.

"Oh, this only started about two weeks ago. I believe he was getting close to solving it."

Trevor made a mental note to go through Richard's desk to see if he found out who was calling Serene. He couldn't believe that he went from having one to three suspects in a matter of minutes.

Trevor felt it was time to change the subject. He didn't want Laurel to feel like she was being investigated, especially under such unfortunate circumstances.

"Thank you for the information, Laurel. As you know, Richard and Serene's funeral is tomorrow. It will be a sad day for all I presume, but I was wondering if I could sit with you and Mark, to help support him?"

"Of course, you can."

Laurel and Trevor talked for a few more hours, even turning a sorrowful situation into a time of laughter as they discussed life, joyous moments, along with watching some family game shows.

"Laurel, I must hand it to you. The pasta was superb. If I could have seconds, I would, but I have to head out. Don't you agree that it was delicious Mark?" Trevor tried to remain as upbeat as possible around Mark in hopes that he would return to the talkative boy, he once was.

Mark only nodded.

"Ha, there you go; the boy even has good taste in food. Hopefully, his future wife cooks as well as you, or he may be disappointed. Well, it was honestly a pleasure spending the day with you and Mark, but I must head out now," he said before placing both hands upon Mark's shoulders. "Mark, don't forget to help Aunt Laurel when she needs it; I am counting on you to do so. I will be visiting you guys again soon, have a great night."

Trevor, Laurel and Mark ended the night on a very special note. By the looks of it, it seemed that everyone would be able to pull through this. Each day, it seemed another life entered the picture, hoping to help mend, the brokenhearted.

Chapter 7

Spring Comes and Spring Goes

The time had come; the time for everyone to say their final goodbyes to Richard and Serene. A lot of people attended their funeral— friends, loved ones and friends of friends. Sheriff Asher and Trevor were taking it the hardest in the unit since they were the closest to Richard; but this is not to say that everyone in attendance was not just as devastated. Everyone talked with one another in hopes of offering consolation during this sad time.

Trevor greeted Chanel with a smile. "Nice to see you, Chanel; and thank you for coming. Your uniform is looking, how may I say it? Extra sharp today."

"Thank you, Trevor, you look nice yourself. This is a tough day," Chanel expressed, trying to keep her emotions from getting the better of her. "Never in a million years would I have guessed we would be burying Richard...never would have..."

"I know, this is hard for us all. Life and death are a sad reality we all must face." He stopped and thought for a minute as he clenched his jaw. "But it should never be in the hands of another man; criminal monsters with no heart or soul." Trevor's thoughts were once more on Haden.

Chanel noticed Trevor was becoming angered, so she decided to lighten the conversation a bit. "Is that your family back there?" She asked, her eyes beaming with joy. "Oh, they are so beautiful. Your children have gotten so big!"

"Yeah, I know; they are growing before my very eyes. It feels like my wife and I have to buy new size clothes every month," said Trevor as he chuckled. "It's really starting to put a dent in my pockets."

All the guests continued to talk with one another. In general, the atmosphere seemed to be alright. Everyone was reconnecting with friends and family they hadn't seen in a long time, consoling one another with reassurance. It wouldn't be much longer before Trevor, spotted Richard's sister, Bertha.

Trevor's eyes shone with glee. "Bertha, I am very sad we have to come together on an occasion such as this, but it is so nice to see you."

"Thank you, Trevor. Richard was really the only one who was always there for me, to reach out to me when I needed somebody to talk to...I miss him so much," said Bertha before breaking down in tears.

Trevor wrapped Bertha in a comforting embrace. "Bertha...Bertha, it's okay. I am sure Richard knows you appreciated him, and I am sure he will remain with you in your heart." Now was Trevor's chance to do some investigating. Despite being at a funeral, his work was never done. Especially since his efforts was for Richard. "So, where is he?"

"Who?"

"You know...Haden." Trevor was almost too disgusted to even mention his name.

"Oh, about that, he said he had important errands to run. I insisted he come, but he had other plans."

Trevor's stomach turned in disgust. Haden didn't even have the decency to show up to his wife's brother's funeral. In his mind, he felt there was a sinister reasoning behind it. "Interesting. So, is it true that Haden and Richard had an argument recently concerning you?"

She sighed a sound that carried the weight of unspoken thoughts and emotions brewing within. The tension in her chest tightened as she considered best, how to respond. "Yes, about three weeks ago. I told Laurel about the situation, so I guess she gave word to Richard about it, though I wanted it to stay between the two of us. Richard was furious when he arrived at my house. The two never liked each other to be honest. It did get rather bad. I'd never seen them argue so intensely until that that day. Haden was playing cards with a friend and if his friend didn't intervene, I believe the two would have fought, or even worse."

Trevor couldn't hold back. "Is it true Haden threatened Richard? If so, what did he say? I need you to tell me everything Bertha, please."

Bertha's eyes widened as they plead with his. "Oh please! Trevor, please! Don't tell me you're thinking Haden killed my brother. The two never liked each other, but I don't believe Haden would do such a thing. "I mean sure, he is short-tempered, but I don't think he would go as far as to murder someone, let alone my brother," said Bertha as tears streamed down her face.

"I know now is not the best time to discuss this, but I will be paying Haden a visit soon for some questioning."

She shook her head in anguish. "Do what you must Trevor."

The funeral began and everyone sat in their desired spots. Police officers from many departments including Trevor's were in attendance.

Some were upfront near the podium, standing at ease during the service to give their respects. The pastor delivered a lengthy and profoundly heartfelt speech that resonated deeply with everyone in attendance. As he spoke, his voice carried a weight of emotion that seemed to envelop the room, inviting attendees to reminisce about shared moments and celebrate the impact he had left behind. There were many people who spoke, including Sheriff Asher and Chanel. They all had nothing but words of respect for Richard and Serene. Those who knew Serene spoke of her loving ways and maternal instincts towards all she knew. Eventually, Trevor stepped out of his seat to go to the podium and give his sincere thoughts on the couple, his friends.

"Richard, Serene, what can I say that hasn't already been said? What words define Richard? Caring, persistent, resilient. The list continues. What words define Serene? Affectionate, wise, maternal, and likewise; the list continues. We gather today not to mourn their departure, but rather to celebrate the times we were able to spend with them. Celebrate the times we were able to learn and grow in their presence. They themselves were an example, so we could go out into the world and be an example to others. I knew Richard since the age of twenty and he always remained the same, meaning he retained his leadership quality, wisdom, and a will to learn. Whenever I was down, he would always be there to pick me up. Whenever I needed advice, he was always there to provide it. Richard leaves behind a part of him, a part of him that will grow up, I believe, to be spectacular. A legacy. Mark, what can I say about him other than that he is a respectable and loveable young man due to his mother's nurturing and upbringing. Sure, Richard was an outstanding guy, but I know Serene helped to bring it out of him. She was his motivation to stay strong.

"Richard would always talk about Serene as if she were hand-delivered by God Himself. If he had a chance to go back and analyze every woman on this earth before choosing Serene, I know for a fact he would not do so. He knew Serene was the perfect wife for him as soon as the two met. His soul said she was the one. When he first met Serene, his soul and manly instincts told him that she was the perfect woman. The perfect woman to grow and nurture with, the perfect woman to love and create a family with. It saddens me and everyone here to say our final goodbyes to Richard and Serene, but they will live on inside of us. All the things we obtained from them will forever be ingrained in our minds and souls, things of wisdom and love. Before I end my speech, I just want to ask that all of us remain strong and continue to live and do that which is right. This is something both Richard and Serene would have wanted. May the two of you rest in paradise. Farewell."

Everyone in the audience was profoundly moved by Trevor's speech. As Trevor peered into the crowd, he could see nods of heads in agreement and smiles of remembrance and of approval. Those who got a chance to speak gave a heartfelt talk that deeply resonated with everyone; that day showed just how much Richard and Serene impacted everyone who knew them.

The time for Richard and Serene to be buried had come. It was only right that they get a side-by-side burial plot and that is just what friends and family got for them. Everyone in attendance took turns placing dirt on their caskets, along with a flower and their last respects. It took quite a while for it to come down to the very last person. No one complained as all cherished the moment; a moment to cherish the lives of two people near and dear to all who were blessed enough to know them.

Trevor was next in line. No matter how hard he tried, he could not contain his tears anymore. He held two flowers in his hands, and before placing them on their caskets, he breathed deeply. "I will miss you guys, rest in paradise." Bending down, he gently placed one flower on each casket with care.

Not too long after the funeral was concluded, Richard and Serene were finally laid to rest. Many in the unit saw that Trevor was once again emotionally torn. He sat by himself mourning the fact that he would never see Richard again.

Chanel decided to talk to him. "Trevor, I know this is a hard thing to accept. Richard is gone, but you two were best of friends and I'm sure he appreciated you dearly. He knows who his friends were, he knows who cared for him. Cherish all the good times you had together and do not forget them. When you remember them, do not let them bring you down. Rather, let them brighten your day and bring joy knowing the great times you all spent together."

"Thanks, Chanel. It's just that I thought I was mentally ready to say goodbye. But once I actually saw the earth cover their caskets, that is when I truly knew it was official that they were gone. It's hard knowing I won't see them again. I'm just thinking about Mark. He'll no longer see his mom and dad's smile, hear their words of encouragement…this is just too much to take in. During the service, just seeing the tears fill his eyes was so hard. I'm just glad his Aunt Laurel was there to console him."

"Trevor, this has been really hard for us all, but as long as we have each other, we will be able to heal emotionally. Just think about how you have been there for families and loved ones of murder victims, how you consoled each one and helped them move on and deal with the situation. Apply those same nurturing words to yourself and those around you. Think positive. Don't let this situation keep you down for the rest of your life. Richard wouldn't want that."

"I know Chanel, but to lose such a close friend is a hard thing. I am sure I will be able to pull through. I think I better go and see what Mark is doing. Laurel is with him, but I'm sure he could use some more support."

"No Trevor, you stay here and pull yourself together. I'm sure you will be of great help to Mark, but you must at the same time think about your own wellbeing. I will go and check on him."

Chanel approached Laurel and Mark. Mark of course didn't seem to be handling the loss of his parents well.

"Hello Laurel, nice to see you again. I just want to thank you for being here for Mark, I am sure your big sister is proud of the way you have stepped up. When Mark looks up at you, I am sure he sees his mother."

"Thank you, officer, those words mean a lot to me. But no one will ever be able to replace Serene. She was one of a kind."

"I see Mark is still taking this pretty hard. It's not surprising. Is it okay if I talk with him for a moment?"

"Please do."

Officer Chanel knelt before Mark to give him words of encouragement. This was hard for anyone of any age to accept, so she could only imagine the struggle it created for a young child. Chanel spoke in a cheerful but calm tone. "Hey Mark, hello, how are you? I'm Officer Chanel, we met before. Remember me?"

Mark sobbed. "Yes."

"Mommy and Daddy were very nice people while they were here. Your mom and dad are in a very special place, a place of happiness and fun. This is a place that nice people go to when they pass. What's better is that the fun will never end."

"You mean where all the angels are? Mommy used to tell me about them."

"Yes Mark, where all the beautiful angels are. Not only are the beautiful angels there, but lovely flowers, beautiful water, and nice people just like your mom and dad."

"If I'm good too, will I see them again?"

"Yes, of course Mark, but a very long time from now. Now I want you to stay strong for Aunt Laurel and not only that, listen and be the good boy that you are, okay? Will you promise to do that for me?"

"Okay," answered Mark as his crying subsided.

"I will be seeing you soon to see how well you're doing," said Chanel, before kissing him on the forehead.

Laurel wrapped her arms around Mark before smiling towards Chanel with gratitude. "Thank you so much Officer for your kind words, which mean a lot to the both of us. You and Trevor continue to be there for each other, that's what friends are for."

"Will do, thank you, and take care."

The majority of those in attendance had already left the premises. Remaining was Trevor, his family, Officer Chanel, and a few other officers. Chanel approached Trevor, his wife, and his kids to leave them with a few words.

"I am heading out now. It was a pleasure seeing you guys again, such a lovely family. Take care."

Trevor stayed a while longer with his family before deciding to leave. Trevor made one more stop at Richard and Serene's grave to give his last goodbyes. Trevor hunched before their grave, his appearance taking on a somber quality as he knelt in the soft earth. "Richard, Serene, if you're listening right now, I know I probably sound like a broken record. But I just want to let you know, again, that I will miss you both dearly. You two touched everyone that happened to be around you guys in such an inspiring way. You guys will always be remembered for the good you did for those around you, for always being selfless and giving. I will make sure I find the person who did this, I promise. Rest in paradise, friends."

The healing process would be a long one for all who knew Serene and Richard. Day by day, step by step, everyone was trying to resume their normal lives. Winter was coming to an end and the arrival of spring was near, a symbol of new beginnings not only for nature, but also for those who were affected by the passing. A new beginning hopefully of joy, progression, motivation and most of all, healing.

* * *

Back at the unit, everything was pretty much back to normal. Still, in the back of everyone's mind was the question of, who did it? And furthermore, why? Now that the grieving process had come to an end, Trevor's main focus was on who committed the crime, and he was determined to find the answer.

Chanel pat Trevor on his shoulder reassuringly. "Good to see you have been holding up pretty well the past few days."

"Yeah, it still gets to me at times, but in general, I've managed to keep composed." Then he voiced what had been on his mind for the past few days, the issue surrounding Richard and Haden. The others tried to keep Richard's investigation concerning Haden out of the topics of conversation, but he had to know. "I've been thinking a lot about this Haden, and I'm pretty sure he had something to do with the murders. I will be paying him a visit soon; I need to bring him in for questioning. I cannot think of anyone else who had a problem with Richard, and overall, that Haden is just an overall bad guy. He treats Richard's sister like crap and it's a real shame. I have no idea why she stays with such scum." Trevor spewed out all his thoughts, taking the moment to recompose himself.

"I know Trevor; I know how you feel. But we can't jump to conclusions and pin such a heinous crime on someone without first making sure it was them. We need evidence to suspect it was him. We are getting there; time and patience are all we need. Remember, we are also looking into the suspicious phone calls Serene was receiving. We haven't gotten through compiling our list of suspects to interview, yet."

Sheriff Asher came out of his office to update Trevor on the next steps. Which was certainly good news to the ears.

"Trevor, I have cleared you to go to Haden's residence and inform him that he must come in for questioning. Tomorrow morning you can go to get him for the questioning. That way, we will have enough time in the day to compile any evidence and analyze statements. Trevor, I can see that you're anxious, but take your time. You have been stressed enough lately. I can assure you we will find the killer; he will not get away by any means. We have a superb detective unit and an outstanding forensic team on our side, we will get to the bottom of this. The rest of the crew and I will help you all along the way."

Trevor's nostrils flared as he stood upright. "Can I go today? Please. Knowing that every second this killer is out breathing and enjoying life while two innocent people are gone, just fills me with wrath. Just the thought is too much for me at times."

"Trevor, listen to me. I need you to keep it professional. Going to his doorstep full of anger won't do us any good. You might provoke him and put yourself, along with citizens in danger. Of course, I will send some backup with you, but I will leave the confrontation in your hands since you insist you be the one to confront him."

Trevor was fuming. He hunched over his desk with his knuckles planted firmly to contain himself. "I won't do anything to make myself or the unit look bad."

Chanel wasn't convinced. She placed down her glass on the table. "Major, let's assume that Haden did in fact kill Richard and Serene. You won't catch him if you let your feelings get in the way. Remember, you have to trip him up so that he admits to what he did. Don't let it be the opposite way around, meaning, do not let him control your emotions."

"I guess you two are right," Trevor responded. Deep down, he already picked out the cell that Haden would rot in. He knew Haden did it. Now he just had to prove it.

Chanel's eyes glistened as they stared intensely into Trevor's. "Okay. Good. It's time to call it a night. Get some rest, Trevor, so you can be at your best for Haden tomorrow."

"Thanks, guys. I will. This case could be solved by this time tomorrow."

* * *

Trevor found it hard to fall asleep as his eagerness to confront Haden was keeping him awake. Trevor felt deep inside that Haden committed the crime; he believed he was at the doorstep of justice, bringing Richard and Serene's killer to judgment to pay for their misdeed. He tried his best to fall asleep, only managing to rest his eyes for minutes a time. He hoped the next time he opened them, the sun would be out so he could head to work and solve the crime once and for all. Trevor managed to fall asleep for about an hour before it was finally time to awake. He decided to skip breakfast and coffee but stuck with the normal routine of kissing his wife and kids' goodbye before leaving.

Chapter 8

If He Forces You to Go One Mile, Go Two with Him

Trevor finally arrived at the station, more ready than ever to pursue Haden. Trevor waited a while longer for Asher to arrive so he could give him the final go-ahead. He paced back and forth impatiently as he waited.

On those occasions when he had a moment to himself, he couldn't help but envelop himself in those "what if" moments. Moments that made him question the act that was committed against his best friend. Questions that made him ask himself over and over, "why Richard?" In those "what if?" moments, he hoped to come closer to solving the murder of his best friend.

As Trevor stood and had one of those moments within the station, he felt a strange, burning sensation on the back of his neck. A feeling that let him know, "someone is definitely behind me". He turned only to find Chanel standing with arms crossed as she gently shook her head.

"Trevor, you are overcomplicating things again, aren't you?"

Trevor somberly held his head down. "…Yea. It's just that, none of this makes sense to me."

"In life, not everything will make sense in the beginning Trevor. Somethings just take time to get to the bottom of, and this is certainly one of those things."

"I understand Chanel, but this is one of those situations where I wish all the answers were laid before me. It is not fair that we must fight so hard, just so that justice can be brought forth. It is not fair I tell you; it is not fair."

"Hey Trevor, calm down," Officer Chanel finally said. She walked towards him before placing a hand on his shoulder. "I know you're ready to go and confront Haden, but patience is key here. The sheriff will be here in a little while. Until he arrives, relax and take a breather."

"Easier said than done. I've been waiting all night for this moment. You don't understand how badly I want to put this guy away." His mind flashed to the image of Richard and Serene's bodies. "Trust me, you do not understand."

"Look, look. Breathe in, breathe out." She inhaled and exhaled to demonstrate. "Save that adrenaline for when you really need it. I understand. I want to lock this guy up as much as you do, but let us go about this the best way possible."

Trevor's shoulders visibly raised and lowered as he inhaled deeply. "That helped a little bit. I just hope Sheriff arrives before my blood pressure starts to rise again."

Her fingertips touched her lips as she chuckled. "Looks as though I should pursue a career as a therapist. I always knew I had it in me."

Trevor's face slightly blushed. "Hahaha, yea I must say, you got it in ya."

Chanel removed her service hat before slicking her hair in a backward motion. "Yea, I guess so," she said playfully.

When the Sheriff arrived a little while later, Trevor couldn't contain his relief.

"Oh, Sheriff, great to see you," he said sheepishly. "I am ready to go right now, just give me the word."

"Trevor, I can see you're anxious. Are you absolutely sure you're prepared to question Haden today?" Sheriff Asher asked, his voice steady yet filled with genuine concern.

"Just waiting on your order. I'm ready when you are." Trevor looked upward, thinking of Richard. "I know he's, our guy; I know it Sheriff."

"Besides looking like you just drank five energy drinks, I suppose you're ready to go. Just remember what we told you. Remain calm and professional. If he is guilty, let him do himself in. More than likely Bertha will also be there when you confront him, so for her safety, be wise. I guess you're good to go."

A sudden sense of dejection came over Trevor. "Of course, Sheriff, of course. Richard would want me to protect his baby sister, not put her in danger. I will try to make the confrontation as non-physical as possible."

Gently smiling, Asher grasped Trevor by the shoulders. "I believe in you Trevor. Now go out there and show him what the Welder Ville unit is made of."

Trevor and an officer from the unit headed out to Haden and Bertha's home. As he drove to the location, he felt a mix of anxiety and optimism. His mind was playing out the possible scenarios and unfortunately, most of them were not so good. Trevor knew Haden could be unpredictable, and in Trevor's state of uncertainty, the two may clash like hot and cold air, resulting in a hurricane-like situation. Trevor rang the doorbell before Bertha answered. He was happy to see her, but at the same time, his focus was on Haden.

"Hi Bertha, nice to see you. Is Haden home? We'd like to ask him a few questions surrounding the murder of Richard."

Trevor heard a loud bang as Haden slammed down his beer bottle. "Who the hell is that?" He shouted from a distance.

"Detective... Detective Trevor," answered Bertha nervously.

"Detective? And who the hell is this, Trevor? You know what! Wait right there!" Haden scooted himself up from the recliner.

Based on Haden's reaction, Trevor felt confrontation was inevitable. He braced himself, preparing for anything that might take place.

"Yeah?" Haden said. "And you're?"

Trevor flashed his badge. "Detective Trevor. Prior to Richard's murder, we were informed that you and Richard had several disputes. We would like to take you in for questioning."

"Me? Being taken in for questioning? You're out of your damn mind! I am not leaving this house, you hear me? I never got along with that idiot Richard, I never did like him, but I would never kill him! Knowing how he was, I'd say he probably deserved it! Now get your black ass off my damn property!"

The smell of beer emanated from his mouth as he spoke, but for Trevor, his words could not be excused.

What did you just say?" Trevor asked, his voice mingled with a noticeable hint of anger that was evident in the tightening of his jaw and the furrowing of his brows.

The inebriated Haden stepped a closer and the smell of beer emanating from his foul mouth grew stronger. "I said get your black ass off my damn property! That's what!"

Trevor closed his eyes and shook his head. "N-no, what was it you said before that?" he asked, his words hanging in the air.

"I said that damn idiot Richard deserved everything that came his way. Now get the—"

Before Haden could get the next syllable out, Trevor clocked him square in the face, causing him to stumble back and fall flat on his bottom.

"Arrest this clown! We will proceed with the questioning at base," said Trevor to his comrade.

* * *

Bertha was extremely nervous, and it showed all over her face. She feared telling Haden to stop, assuming he would become more aggressive towards her, possibly complicating the situation.

Trevor was enraged beyond control. He placed his hands on his holster as if to take hold of his pistol. It took every ounce of willpower to restrain himself from doing the worst to Haden.

"No! No!" Bertha said. "Please, Trevor, don't hurt him. He is drunk, he doesn't know what he is doing. Trevor, please I am begging you, don't do anything to hurt him."

Seething with rage, Trevor breathed in and out heavily as he stared Bertha in the eyes. "Why do you stay with this guy? Do you know that your brother may have possibly died fighting for you to leave him? Yet, you remain with him. We'll bring him to the station to let him sober up and then we'll begin questioning."

"Just go," Bertha answered as she sobbed.

Back in the squad car, Haden continued to berate Trevor and the other officer with obscene language.

"We got you now, buddy," Trevor said as he drove down the road. "You will pay for what you did, I can guarantee you of that."

Haden laughed smugly. "Shut up, you piece of shit. Clearly birds of the same feather do flock together because you and that good for nothing Richard obviously knew each other. The idiot is gone and now you've taken his place, just great."

Trevor slammed the brakes and pulled the car to the side of the road before giving Haden a grim warning. The officer present with Trevor had never seen this side of him; even he feared for Haden. Trevor reached over the back seat, grabbing Haden by his shirt.

"I promise, if you say one more word about Richard, it will be your last word. Do you hear me?" said Trevor seething.

Haden fell silent. Trevor unclenched his fist, causing Haden to fall back into the seat with a thud. Releasing his grip, he began to recompose himself so that he could bring Haden to justice the lawful way. They proceeded to the department to bring the immature, foul-mouthed Haden to justice. It seemed Trevor's warning penetrated all the booze that filled Haden's head since he didn't say another word.

They arrived at the station and Haden was finally taken in to be questioned.

"This nut again," one of the officers said in passing. "It seems he can't do without us. It's almost as if he makes it his duty to come here."

"I'll bring him into the interrogation room where he'll sit for a while longer, just to clear his mind and get sober. Then I'll start with the interrogation and finally get the truth from this monster."

"He looks pretty bruised," Officer Chanel said.

"Yeah, I'm sure he deserved it," Sheriff Asher responded, choosing to ignore the rules that Trevor broke when he punched him. "It actually may have been long overdue."

Trevor and the rest waited about two hours before proceeding with the interrogation. Hopefully enough time had passed for Haden to sober up and become approachable. Corporal Maribel was updated on the situation when she arrived.

Trevor and the sheriff walked into the room where Haden was being held to conduct the questioning.

"Haden, Haden, Haden," Trevor said, pacing slowly back and forth in front of him. "On the night of March 4th, where were you around two a.m.?"

"I was out hanging with my friends," Haden answered curtly.

"Where were you hanging out?"

"I really shouldn't be answering any crap you ask me because I know I am innocent. The fact that you even assume it was me who did the crime shows how much of a lowlife you are." Haden had apparently recovered from Trevor's threat from earlier as he became emboldened once more.

"I'm sure everyone here agrees there is only one lowlife currently present and it sure isn't me. I'm going to ask you again; can you describe the type of location you were at? Do you remember the name?"

"I was at Bubba's Stack Shack. I had some food to eat and I drank a bit. Are you happy now?"

"Approximately how long did you stay there?"

"I don't know, maybe a little over an hour. I'd say from about one a.m. till two or three-ish."

"Interesting, and where did you go after leaving?"

"Where do you think, Sherlock? Home."

"Did you go straight there, or did you detour?"

"Straight there. Look, I'm not about to sit here answering silly questions all day. That idiot Richard leaves and here you're, to take his place, just awesome. The gift that keeps on giving."

Sheriff Asher stood in the corner of the room while Trevor conducted the interrogation. He could tell Haden was getting to him emotionally and so he stepped in before it got out of hand.

Asher outstretched his hands before his comrade. "Trevor, don't do it. Let him make a fool out of himself."

Trevor squinted. "But did you not hear what he just said? Like, I am really tired of hearing this guy."

"Yes, I heard it loud and clear, but as I told you before, you can't give fools the impression they are winning."

Trevor took a deep breath. "I guess the interrogation is over. I have gathered enough information to investigate the area. I'm sure the surveillance cameras in the place he speaks of will either prove or disprove his claim."

"So can I go now for crying out loud?" Haden snarled. Fed up, he threw his hands in the air. "Can I?"

"Take him to the front to be cleared," said Asher to a nearby officer.

Haden was escorted out of the room, free for now. Trevor was hoping Haden was lying just so he could send him to jail for the rest of his days. Trevor didn't want to waste any time in proceeding to the area in question to investigate.

"Sheriff, why stall any longer? I say let's investigate Bubba's Stack Shack right now and ask to look at the tapes. I promise, if it is shown he was not at the property at the time he says he was, or at all, I will personally throw him in jail myself."

"He is all yours from here on out if so."

"Let's get going."

Sheriff and Trevor headed in their squad car to Bubba's Stack Shack to obtain the surveillance footage from the manager. During the drive, the two decided to speak further regarding the series of events.

"Speaking of surveillance, I wish Richard's was working before the murder. I know he usually had it working and he spoke to me before he passed about fixing it. I guess he was just too busy to do it in time. If only it had been working, then we would be able to at least see the perpetrator for sure."

"No point thinking about what-ifs," said Sheriff Asher. "It will not bring Richard and Serene back. Our main focus now is to find who did this crime and bring them to justice. Outside distractions will only hinder that process."

"You're right. Let's stay focused on the task at hand. We could be on our way to solving the crime right now. I know it's Haden. He's scum. It has to be him."

"We can't jump to conclusions. Innocent until proven guilty. Besides, we still have the neighbor that went AWOL and the mystery phone caller. I have the others gathering as much information as they can back at the station. We need to have other options ready, in case Haden isn't the one."

"You're right, sheriff. Oh, great, it looks like we've arrived. It's right there, around the corner."

Trevor and Sheriff Asher were soon at Bubba's Stack Shack, a piece to a puzzle they hoped, would soon be solved.

"Good afternoon," the host said. "Table for two?"

"No thank you. I'm Detective Trevor and this is Sheriff Asher. We would like to speak to your manager if possible."

"Okay, give me one moment," said the host as she stepped away.

Trevor sniffed the air. "It smells great in here. Once we lock up Haden, the station should come here to celebrate right before, or after we rub it in his face."

Sheriff Asher grabbed Trevor's arm and pulled him to the side. "Trevor, look at me. Remember, we must stay focused. Like I told you before, don't jump the gun, we must have reason to believe he is guilty. It is not ethical to deem Haden the perpetrator just because you have ill feelings towards him."

Huffing, Trevor struggled to accept Asher's advice. "Okay sheriff, I hear you." Trevor peered over the Sheriff's shoulder enthusiastically. "Great, it looks like the manager has arrived."

Puzzled, the manager approached. "Hi, so how may I help you guys? I heard you're detectives?"

"Yes, in fact, we are," Trevor answered. "We have a person of interest in a murder case who claims he was here, when a murder was committed. If we can prove that to be true, we will no longer have any reason to believe him to be involved."

"Man, sorry to hear that. A murder of any kind is terrible, especially if undeserved. Follow me, I will obtain the tape for you."

They followed the manager to the backroom to obtain evidence that may possibly solve the murder mystery once and for all.

"If I am wrong about suspecting Haden of this murder, I won't feel any regrets," Trevor said.

"For him to threaten Richard was a crime in itself; he is lucky it was not reported when it first happened."

"Here you go guys," said the manager as he handed over the tape. "Good luck on finding the killer, or, killers. I hope they are brought to justice soon."

"Thank you. We will surely find them," Sheriff Asher said before he and Trevor walked away. They hoped and believed that what they had in their possession would lead to closure.

Chapter 9
Decisive Moment

Trevor and Asher took the squad car back to the department, excited to analyze the tape. Whether Haden was lying or telling the truth, either way the tape would allow them to focus their attention elsewhere. If he was telling the truth, Trevor could finally think about the other possible suspects. If he was lying, they would be one step closer to arresting Richard's murderer.

* * *

Back at home, Haden was still furious that he was a suspect in the case.

"Why in the hell would they think I killed Richard? Why?" said Haden furiously before tossing a bottle of beer across the room which shattered on impact.

"I don't know hon. I guess they are just assuming a lot of people are suspects. I'm sure you're not the only one under suspicion."

"You're trying to be a smart ass, aren't you! You really think I am going to believe that 'let's just assume he's a suspect' crap? Also, how did Trevor and everyone else know about the argument Richard and I had not too long ago? Did you open your damn big mouth?" Haden lumbered toward her; his fists balled.

Bertha held her hands towards him as she cowered in fear. "No, please, just stop. You're scaring me."

"You're damn right, you better be scared. You're lucky they have their eyes on me already, because otherwise, I would let your ass have it. I know you spoke to them! Let anyone know about our personal business again and you will regret it. Do you hear me? Do you hear me!"

"Yes! Okay!" Bertha said as she wept.

"Coming in my house disrespecting me like that, the nerve of him. I know Richard was your brother, but he has always been a jerk to me. You know he meant no good for us."

"Look, do not bring my brother up anymore, you hear me? I am getting sick and tired of you! Okay? Don't do it again!"

"Or what? Or what? What are you going to do, leave me? You know you have nobody else, so go ahead, be stupid if you want. I'm not going to lie to anyone here. Your brother was a jerk who just stayed in our business all day. I said it before and I will say it again, your brother was a jerk. Your. Brother. Was. A. Jerk."

The moment he said this, Haden's face was showered with spit as he stood stunned. He was always used to Bertha standing down to his barrage of insults. Now that she had stood up for herself, he was left bemused as to how to answer it.

"I told you, I am tired of you!" Bertha shouted. "Keep messing with me and it is you who will be getting buried. Do you hear me? I am sick of you! Maybe it was you who killed my brother after all! Here I was all this time defending such a monster, denying the fact that you would stoop so low. Now that I think of it, you're very capable of doing such a thing. Listen closely and listen well, do not mess with me anymore. I refuse to sit here and listen to you disrespect the dead! Leave my brother alone, do you hear me?" Bertha trembled with anger as she sternly aimed her finger towards his face.

Haden wiped the saliva off his face and said nothing, watching as Bertha angrily walk away.

* * *

Back at the station, everyone gathered around to analyze the video.

"It's good to see you guys are making strides in solving this," Corporal Maribel said.

"I think he's the one," Trevor added as he grinned. "Even if this evidence proves him innocent, it still won't change my perception of him, which is that he is an inconsiderate scumbag who has no regard for anyone but himself."

Asher crossed his arms as he raised his eyebrows. "Well, the insane asylum is another option if he is proven innocent."

"I doubt even they would want him," Trevor responded. "Chanel should almost be finished setting up the footage and fast-forwarding to the specific timestamp in question."

"We are set up and ready to go," Officer Chanel said as she entered the room. Everyone was excited and nervous at the same time.

"According to the forensic team, their deaths occurred at approximately three a.m.," Trevor said. "Let's look at time stamps ranging from one a.m. to four a.m."

"Okay, let me fast forward." Chanel looked at the footage intently. "So far, nothing suspicious."

"Keep going, something should come up soon," Sheriff Asher said. "Wait! There! There! Rewind it a bit."

"I think I saw it too, but there is no guarantee that was Haden," Chanel answered as she studied the footage. "Let's take a look. Hmmm...I see a group of people, but none of them look like Haden. Let's keep fast-forwarding."

"Just a while longer," Corporal Maribel chimed in.

"Stop here, who is that guy coming out of the car?" Trevor asked. "Keep letting it play."

"Nothing...nothing.... wait, there!" Chanel pointed full of optimism. "This is definitely Haden. So, he is spotted at 2:21 a.m. and he appears to be exiting a vehicle with friends."

"Okay, so he was telling the truth about being there," Trevor said. "But we still have to see what time he leaves the location."

"This should be easier to determine. Let me fast forward a bit, ah! There! He leaves at 4:01 a.m. I think Haden has officially been cleared as a suspect. Even if he was to leave here and go to Richard's residence, it is a considerable drive."

"Well, Trevor, I guess Haden was telling the truth after all," Sheriff Asher said. "Now, we can focus our attention elsewhere and come closer to solving this."

"Man, I really thought he was the guy," Trevor said solemnly. "I guess I was wrong for accusing him without enough proof, but as I said before, I still don't like the guy."

"At least we are slowly but surely getting closer to solving this case." Chanel walked forward as she gently grasped Trevor by his hands.

"No sense in focusing on this anymore," Corporal Maribel exclaimed. "Let's move on, there is more work to be done. We found out the name of Serene's mystery caller, he is identified as Colton Reed. Trevor, you were right; Richard was investigating him. It looks like he found his address and was planning to confront him before…"

Trevor knew what she was about to say, as he sadly answered. 'Before he was murdered.'

"I'll go question him." Trevor looked at the address written on the piece of paper Corporal Maribel handed him. "Wow, he's just in the town over. This could be our guy." Trevor felt a mixture of excitement and anger at the thought of finally catching Richard and Serene's killer.

* * *

It took Trevor about forty-five minutes to reach the address. This time, Chanel traveled along with him. They had decided that he might be more receptive to a woman if things went south, considering this guy had been stalking Serene.

They pulled up to a slightly run-down row of apartments. After a quick survey of its surroundings, they approached Colton's residence.

Chanel squinted as she got a close look at the door. "Unit B, here it is."

Anxiety kicked in as Chanel knocked on the door; but it would not be long before she recomposed herself. They could hear rustling inside as they awaited a response. A man finally answered the door dressed in pajama pants, exhibiting considerable heavy bags under his eyes. Trevor found this unusual since it was the afternoon. But inside the apartment, things looked rather pristine. There was a fresh lemon scent that Trevor could only guess was the smell of cleaning products.

"Uh, hello. Can I help you?" Colton seemed nervous as he eyed Trevor and Chanel's badges.

"Are you Colton Reed, sir?" Trevor asked. His hand rested on the handcuffs in his back pocket.

"Uh, yes, I am."

"Colton, we have evidence that shows that you made multiple phone calls to the residence of Serene and so—" Colton cut Trevor off before he could finish.

"Oh jeez. Oh, jeez! Yes, yes, I am so embarrassed. I tried to call to apologize, but the phone was disconnected." Colton ran his fingers through his hair. His cheeks were flushed with embarrassment.

"What do you mean you were embarrassed, sir? We have reason to believe you were harassing this woman."

"Harassing? No. I would never." He paused to take a breath. "Would you like to come in? I can explain everything."

Trevor and Chanel looked toward one another before they cautiously entered the apartment. There wasn't much in it, but the things that were had clearly been recently cleaned and dusted.

Colton saw that they wouldn't be taking a seat any time soon, so he began his account of the event. "You see, I recently got a divorce. It's been really hard on me because my wife got custody of the kids and they moved to Florida." He paused as if he still felt the sting of the events. "I was in really bad shape. I started drinking a lot and…I guess I got to thinking about the past. See, Serene and I went to the same high school. We dated for two years. And, you see, I got really sentimental a couple nights and decided to give her a call. I-I-I don't know what I was thinking and apparently, my drunk self didn't either because I always ended up hanging up when she asked my name."

Trevor and Chanel looked at each other. Should they believe him?

One question loomed on the mind of Chanel as she squinted. "How were you able to obtain their phone number?"

Colton breathed a sigh of shame. "I was able to find her on social media. She was friends with one of my friends. From there, I was able to get her number. I tried messaging her there, but it seemed like she hadn't used her account in a while."

"So, she had her number posted on her page," Chanel prodded.

Colton rested his fingers on his head. *What did I get myself into?* "No, but on her page, she had one picture of what I presumed was her and her husband. In the caption, she wrote something like, 'Mr. and Mrs. Addison'. I decided to search her name in the public records and only three women came up with that first and last name within the 50 miles. I decided I would try all three. By the second try, I knew immediately it was her just by her voice on the answering machine. I knew she was married based on the post she made on her page. I wasn't trying to get in the way of that. As I said earlier, I just went through a difficult breakup, and she was my first crush and I just felt I needed to hear her voice. Again, I am sorry for the trouble I may have caused."

A brief but awkward silence ensued as Colton paused.

Colton continued. "I'm so embarrassed, honestly, I am. I eventually decided to see a therapist and I have been coping a lot better with the divorce. My therapist told me to make this apartment my new home by respecting it. So, I coped with the loneliness by cleaning every day, and I gave up drinking for a while. I tried to call Serene to apologize; it must have been scary to get those calls…But when I called to apologize, the phone was disconnected. Would you guys be able to tell her I am sorry for the trouble I caused?"

Trevor sighed as great dejection came about. "Unfortunately, Serene is dead, sir."

Colton looked as if the wind was knocked out of him. "Wh-what? No. How?"

Trevor could not help but sympathize as Colton begin to cry. "It looks like she was the casualty in a murder meant for someone else. Even though we didn't believe she was the intended target, we still needed to investigate anyone who might wish her harm. You tell an elaborate tale, but if you can't prove your whereabouts for the day of March 4th, we can't rule you out as a suspect."

"March 4th you say?" Colton's sobbing had reduced to whimpers as he got up and went over to his desk. "I was in Florida that day, signing the divorce papers. I can show you the date on the papers and the receipt from the hotel I stayed in while I was there. Do you want to call my ex-wife to confirm?"

Trevor and Chanel looked over the paperwork and receipt that Colton had given them. Chanel noticed that Trevor didn't say anything so she spoke up "No, sir, these will suffice. Thank you for your cooperation."

* * *

Trevor and Chanel arrived back at the station. Trevor had been quiet the entire ride there. He was once again disappointed that they hadn't found Richard's killer and brought him to justice. Trevor wished that he could have told Serene, that they figured out who was giving the mysterious calls, that way with the help of her husband Richard, Serene would have been happy to have helped Colton through such a difficult time. That's just the type of person she was.

Chanel relayed the information they found about the case to her colleagues while Trevor collected himself. She would come back a few minutes later with good news for Trevor.

"Trevor, take a look at this. We got the background check report back for Ben Warren. It turns out that Richard and Ben had to go to court over a dispute about their fence. Ben thought that Richard's fence was too far on to his property line. Therefore, they went to court to settle it, and it appears that Richard won. If what the neighbor told us about Ben was right, perhaps he was angry about losing the case. Therefore, having a motive to kill Richard. He's also close enough to get in and get out within the timeframe of the murder."

Trevor's hope was restored. Perhaps they would catch Richard's killer today. "It is certainly suspicious that he would flee to Spain for some unknown reason. Has anyone been able to contact him in Spain? Is he back in the country?"

Chanel nodded. "Actually yeah. A coworker called and said that he was at work today."

"Well, let's go get our guy!" Trevor said enthusiastically.

"Innocent until proven guilty," Chanel sang out as she followed him to the car.

* * *

When they reached Ben's work, the coworker who called directed Trevor and Chanel to his desk. A slender man was nodding off in the cubical. Trevor cleared his throat loud enough to stir the man awake.

"Oh, um, sorry. Can I help you?" Ben asked startled. He looked sad and tired.

"Ben Warren?" Chanel prodded.

"Yes, that's me." Ben didn't look surprised to see them. His coworkers must have told him that the station was looking for him.

"We have a few questions about your whereabouts in the early morning of March 4th. Do you have an alibi sir?"

"Oh, is this about Richard and his wife? Poor guy, I am so sorry to hear of their passing. It's really a tragedy."

"We heard that you and Richard didn't get along," Trevor chimed in.

"We had our disputes as any neighbors do. It's hard to share adjoining properties and not get into arguments. We went to court once over the fence line. But the court ruled in his favor, and I had to respect that. It wasn't worth killing the guy over." Ben's voice got a little shaky at the end as it finally dawned on him that he was a suspect in a murder case.

"So, where were you on the morning of the murder?" Trevor asked as he eyed Ben suspiciously.

"I was on a plane to Spain. My grandfather called me and told me my grandmother was sick in the hospital. She had been sick for a while but this time, he didn't know if she would make it. My wife and I hopped on the first plane we could get and thankfully, got to spend our last days with her…She died a few days after we arrived." Ben's eyes watered.

Empathy emanated through Chanel's eyes. "So why didn't your job know all of this? They only said that you left the country in a hurry. I do not mean to sound insensitive about your grandmother, but can you prove any of your claims?"

"Uh, um, yeah. I came straight to work from the airport so here is the ticket. It has the time stamp of when we purchased the ticket which was that night before the murder. And then…" he pulled out his phone and held up a picture. "This is the last picture I have with my grandmother in the hospital. You can see the time stamp here," he said as he pointed. Ben must have been starting to get annoyed that he had to explain that his grandmother died as he added with frustration, "You can look up her obituary online. The funeral was yesterday and then I had to rush back for this crap job."

Chanel gave Trevor a look that said, 'This isn't our guy. His story checks out.'

Trevor sighed. "No need. Sorry for your loss sir. And we are sorry we had to come down here and disturb you. We understand how difficult it is to lose someone. Richard and I were good friends, so I guess I got a little bit of tunnel vision when it came to solving this case."

"I appreciate your apology. Richard was a good person. I hope you find the guy."

Chapter 10

Time Has Prepared Them Well

T he team got back to doing their normal investigative work, which included work outside of the Richard and Serene case. With no new suspects, they had hit a wall in the investigation. But there were plenty of other cases that also needed attention.

Everyone chimed in, utilizing their expertise and experience in keeping things moving smoothly within the department. The rest of the day progressed normally enough, and after a long day's work, everyone was ready to head home.

Chanel tried to stay positive as she reminded everyone to look on the bright side of things. "We weren't able to solve Richard's case, but we were able to close a lot of other cases today. I say we all give ourselves a well-deserved pat on the back."

"I agree," Sheriff Asher added, trying to be nice to Chanel's never-failing positivity. "I'll see you guys tomorrow. It's late and about time that I hit the road."

In agreement, Chanel smiled. "Have a safe trip."

* * *

When Trevor woke up the next morning, he was not feeling well mentally. In a matter of days, they went from having three suspects to none. He decided to take the day off and get his mind together.

"Trevor just called in, he won't be making it in today," Officer Timothy relayed to his colleagues. "He stated he is taking some time off to relax."

Asher rubbed his head and huffed as he slightly smirked. "I was wondering when that guy was going to take a day off; it is much needed. We still have work to do whether we are down one or five men. Let's keep moving."

Chanel rushed towards Asher; concern written on her face. "Sheriff, the forensic scientist is on the phone, he wants to speak with you. It seems important."

Asher dropped what he was doing and scampered to the phone; he knew that when a forensic scientist called, they were usually one step away from solving a case. Forensics had been set back in their case analyses due to a power outage. They must finally be back up and running and tackling the pile of cases that had been put on hold due to the inconvenience. In this instance, he hoped it pertained to Richard and Serene.

"Sheriff speaking."

"We have the fingerprint results from Richard's gun. We know who the killer is," the forensic specialist on the other end blurted out. A gut-wrenching pause ensued. "I'm sorry we have to break this news to you, but you will not like it."

Asher removed his glasses from his face. "What do you mean, I will be sorry? That sounds like a good thing. We can close the case."

In the background, Officer Chanel and a few others watched as Sheriff Asher spoke on the phone with the forensic scientist. His facial expression shifted from pure excitement to heartbreak and utter shock. They watched as the conversation ended, and the phone dropped out of his hands and onto the floor. Sheriff Asher stumbled to a nearby chair and collapsed into it. The team quickly reacted to the alarming sight, rushing to his side with urgency.

"Sheriff! Sheriff!" Officer Chanel shouted. "Talk to me. What's wrong?"

Officer Timothy leaned forward over Asher's desk. "Man, say something! What is the matter?"

Asher managed to compose himself. He picked up the phone from the ground, his face clammy. "Go tell Corporal to come to the office. I want her to be here when I break the news."

Officer Chanel ran as fast as she could and informed Corporal Maribel.

"What is it?"

"I don't know, but it seems pretty serious," Officer Chanel responded.

The two made their way to the office. "Asher, what's the matter?"

Asher looked toward the ceiling. He pressed his lips together to contain his emotions. "You guys, take a seat; I have something very shocking to tell you. The—" A deep breath was taken once more. "The forensic team identified the fingerprints that were located on the handgun. Someone who I, and I am sure you guys, in a million years, would never expect them to belong to..."

Sheriff Asher repeated what he was told and soon everyone was in a state of shock. Faces became pale, eyes watered, and hands began to tremble.

"But why?" Asked Chanel as she stood mortified. "Why would he do such a thing?"

"Dear...this is too much," responded Maribel. Still wanting to stick to the facts, she kept composed. "We will get the answers we need when we question him." She paused and shook her head as if it would wake her from the horrible nightmare. "Just when we thought the case couldn't get any worse, now here it is. Oh, this is too much to bear."

* * *

At home, Trevor was taking the day off to spend quality time with his family. He walked with his wife and children to the nearby park to enjoy the scenery. The day couldn't be described as anything other than sublime. The pizza they ate was exceptionally wonderful, the cheese-like elastic, the sauce semi-sweet and the crust baked to perfection. Trevor and his wife sat on a bench enjoying their slices while watching their children play; spring was in full effect and the flowers had blossomed into their perfection. There was no better day to take off, everything was just perfect.

They spent most of the day outside enjoying the atmosphere. Every moment felt exceptional that day for some reason. Well into the night, the sensation continued; the air was calm and cool, and the home was relaxed. The children fell asleep easily after the fun day they had, a perfect ending to a beautiful day. Trevor and Nadine went to bed to get some much-needed rest.

The next morning, Trevor rose with the sun. If he could have taken another day off to spend with his family, he would have. But he knew he had a job to do, a case to solve. He performed his normal morning routine and headed off to work.

After a nice, stress-free ride, Trevor entered the station and immediately knew something was wrong. He felt uneasy. All eyes were on him, many looking at him with disappointment and regret; he didn't know how to respond to the stares. As the looks of shame intensified around him, a palpable tension filled the air, and he began to feel an overwhelming sense of unease creeping into his very core. The weight of judgment rested heavily upon his shoulders, each pair of eyes boring into him like piercing arrows, amplifying his discomfort with every passing moment.

"How could he," someone said under their breath as he made his way to Sheriff's office.

Another officer stared at Trevor as her eyes brimmed with tears. "Of all people, why? Richard loved him," she stated under her breath.

Trevor's heart began to race as he knew something was wrong, all eyes were focused on him.

Asher peered at Trevor with profound shame. "Trevor, come with me," he said regrefully. "I need to speak to you."

Trevor became increasingly anxious, his heart racing uncontrollably in response to the mounting uncertainty that surrounded him. "Yes, what is it? Did something happen?" he asked, his voice trembling.

Asher continued to stare at him with discomfort and unspeakable shame. "The forensic team called and provided us with the fingerprints that were on Richard's handgun."

Instantly, Trevor's pupils dilated, his heart raced, and his thoughts scattered in every direction.

"Well, what did they say?" said Trevor nervously as his throat descended into his chest. His hands became clammy as his eyes darted nervously about the room, before locking onto Asher's once more.

"The fingerprints, they belonged... This is so hard to say. They belong—" Asher closed his eyes as if flinching at a baseball hurtling toward his face. He finally blurted out what he was trying to say. "They belong to Mark. Mark's fingerprints were discovered on the handgun," said Sheriff Asher, getting chills just mentioning it.

This time, it was like that baseball hurtled right into Trevor's heart. "Mark? Mark, as in Richard's son Mark? No way, but...why?" Trevor got up from his chair and paced the room. "I can't believe this. I personally questioned Mark about that night myself on many occasions. His answers were always odd and short, but I never thought he was capable of doing this."

Asher breathed in deeply as he nodded. "I understand."

Shaking his head as he gazed towards the ceiling, Trevor regathered his thoughts. "I must now admit, deep down inside and in the back of my mind, I always thought there was the possibility he may have done it. But just the thought that he would kill his parents...I can't come to grips with it," said Trevor in utter disbelief.

"All of us here are just as surprised as you, Trevor. We have to question Mark in-depth as to what exactly happened that day and immediately. I say tomorrow we bring him in, and then you and I will speak with him. I have the utmost respect for you Trevor, and when you asked us not to question Mark, I gladly obliged. I know how much Mark means to you. All that matters is that we now have DNA evidence that links us to the suspect. This is not to say Mark murdered his parents. We have to question him first Trevor. Don't feel any differently about Mark until we get all the facts."

The team could barely function after such news. Trevor called Laurel to inform her of the details and told her that Mark must be brought in for questioning.

The next day, Aunt Laurel brought Mark to the department to be questioned. Laurel briefly met with Trevor to ask the surety of the claims.

Aunt Laurel shook her head furiously, petitioning for another possible result. "Are they a hundred percent certain they were his fingerprints? This has to be some kind of mistake."

"We will only know the full details once we have questioned him," Trevor said, trying to stay as impartial as possible.

Trevor talked to Mark before the questioning in order to prepare him mentally to tell all.

"Mark, sit here for a moment. In a few minutes, you will be taken into a room to be asked a few questions. I need you to be absolutely honest with me concerning what you saw that day; there are no ifs, ands, or buts. What happened to your parents was a very serious thing and we want to make sure we know as much as possible about why it happened. I am going to need you to be completely honest with me," said Trevor as he looked him directly in the eyes.

Mark looked scared and uneasy. He immediately put his head down and nodded in agreement. Trevor told Sheriff Asher they were ready to begin questioning. Trevor escorted him into a room where it was just them, Sheriff Asher, and a tape recorder for documentation.

Asher placed his hand on Mark's fragile shoulder. "Today we have a very serious matter to discuss, and I need you to be completely truthful. Whether we are here for a long time or not, is up to you. On the day when Trevor found you hiding in the basement, did you explain to him why you were there?"

"No," said Mark sadly.

"Okay. Well, explain it to us now, Mark." Asher tried not to scare Mark but needed to stay firm. He knew that Trevor had a soft side for Mark, so he had to play bad cop today.

"I was scared."

"What were you scared of Mark?"

"The noises."

"What noises?" Asher and Trevor looked at each other confused.

"They were loud, and mommy and daddy wouldn't get up."

"Okay, Mark, now be honest with me. Did you recently get a hold of your dad's gun?"

Mark moved uneasily in his seat, clearly distressed. His eyes redden as they prepared to shed tears. He fidgeted and squeezed at the bottom of his shirt, balling it up, then releasing it. He looked up at Trevor in tears. Sheriff Asher stopped and looked over at Trevor, sorrowfully shaking his head.

"Did you, Mark?" Trevor prodded.

"Yes!" cried Mark.

Sheriff Asher sighed. "Mark, tell us everything that happened that day."

Mark cried and agreed to tell them everything.

Chapter 11

Pardonable Sin

It was 3:15 a.m. and Serene and Richard were fast asleep. Mark was in his bed where he developed a sudden urge to grab an early morning snack. He went into his parents' room to ask for something to eat. Seeing as they both were fast asleep; he was afraid to wake them.

Mark made his way down the stairs to see if there was any food within his reach. Upon doing so, he noticed his dad's coat was on the table in the living room. Finding this unusual, he attempted to hang it up, despite his obvious height disadvantage. As Mark tried to lift his dad's coat, he noticed his father's handgun was still in the pocket. In the past, Mark had seen his father's gun, though Richard would have preferred he hadn't. Since Mark was curious about what it was, Richard felt he had no choice but to explain it to him. Richard taught Mark about the dangers of guns at a very young age, and he knew they should not be played with.

Knowing the gun's dangers, Mark picked up the weapon and brought it upstairs to his dad. As Mark entered his parents' bedroom, he called out.

"Dad! Dad!" said Mark quietly as to not startle them. Mark called his father for a few more moments. "Dad." But Richard was in a deep sleep. Mark began to shake and nudge Richard, but unfortunately, the hand he shook Richard with was also the hand holding the gun. Mark kept shaking Richard in an attempt to awaken him when suddenly, the gun discharged. Richard was instantly killed as the bullet struck and pierced his heart. Mark was terrified by the sound of the firearm and even more terrified by what he may have just done.

He dropped the weapon onto the blanket. Mark noticed his mom was moving on the other side of the blanket, but he was unaware that the same bullet that just killed his father was also taking his mother's life. Oblivious to the fact that she had been struck, he ran to the other side of the bed. That was when he saw that his mother was in great distress. She turned around, trying to summon her strength as she reached out to him, blood seeping from the corner of her mouth. It was then that Mark realized, she had been hurt. The sight was unbearable. He ran, crying in great agony to the basement. When Mark and his dad played hide and seek, this was always the first place Mark would hide.

At 5:50 a.m. Mark was still hiding under a sheet in the basement. Trapped by fear, he heard footsteps and other noises above him, intensifying his distress. Unbeknownst to him, he was hearing his parents' ghostly footsteps; Richard and Serene were unaware that they had left their bodies due to the tragic accident. Mark continued hiding, all the while hearing his parents walk throughout the house in search of their son, Mark. At one point, he heard his mom's faint voice right in front of him, calling his name.

"Mark...Mark," she cried desperately.

Mark knew it was his mother's voice, but he was also innately aware that it was her spirit reaching out to him. He wanted to respond but fear of the unknown and the fact that he would be responding to her spirit paralyzed him with fear even more.

As Mark hid, he suffered through the agony of knowing what he just done; fear and regret kept him contained in the isolated, cold, damp corner. He continued hearing noises throughout the house, objects turning over and faint voices as his parents searched for their son. This went on until Trevor arrived at their residence, and Mark could finally find some solace and comfort in Trevor's presence.

* * *

Mark finished recounting the events of that awful night and morning. Trevor and Asher felt nothing but sympathy and remorse for him.

Trevor leaned against the wall as the recount took a toll on him. "Poor kid. He was only trying to do the right thing by giving Richard his service weapon because he thought it was not properly stored."

Mark was an emotional wreck. Trevor and Asher felt he had said enough and had him escorted to another area.

"Richard...I know he was always a very careful guy, especially dealing with his firearm," Sheriff Asher said. "Just this one mistake cost two people their lives. Three in fact, because who knows if Mark will recover from this. He only tried to do the right thing, very sad."

"Richard must have forgotten to remove his firearm from his jacket when he got home. I knew we shouldn't have stayed out so late; he was probably exhausted," said Trevor, consumed by grief and regret.

"Mark's statement basically matches up with what the forensic team said. Even sadder is that Mark also mentions hearing his mom and dad's voice even after they had passed...his mind must have been trying to cope with the ordeal and as a result, imagined their voices to give comfort. Poor kid" voiced Asher before placing a hand on Trevor's shoulder. "And no one is to blame here."

"This explains why the bullet was fired at an awkward angle. I guess we have officially closed the case...To know it was done all in innocence, trying to protect his family and do the right thing...I can't even imagine..."

Asher patted Trevor on the back. "Let's go Trevor, no point in dwelling on it now."

Trevor and Asher explained the details to Chanel and Maribel. Everyone was equally shocked as they could not help but feel sympathy for Mark. Knowing that he accidentally took his parents' life would forever be embedded in Mark's conscience. Trevor promised that he would always be there for Mark, to ensure that Mark has a normal childhood as possible, under such circumstances.

"Poor kid, I can only imagine what he is going through," Officer Chanel said. "I am just glad his Aunt Laurel was there to quickly step into his life and take him in. He needs all the support he can get."

"Definitely, anyone who is willing to help, let them," Trevor responded. "The more support Mark receives, the better. Sheriff is in the other room talking with his Aunt Laurel right now; she is devastated by the account. I have never seen her this emotional. When we first told her Mark's fingerprints were found on the weapon, she didn't believe us. It was clear she was just as surprised as we were.

When Mark admitted that he was the one who accidentally took his parents' lives, Laurel became distraught."

A tear trailed down Chanel's cheek. "God help us all."

Trevor entered the room where the sheriff was speaking with Laurel. She was still in tears with her head buried in her lap, weeping intensely at the news. The sheriff was standing over her, gently rubbing her shoulder to give solace.

"It was an accident. Mark is still a great kid; he only meant to do right. With the proper therapy and cooperation, everyone will be able to cope and move on," said Asher to Laurel.

Laurel was too emotional to respond, but she was taking in everything she was being told. Sheriff Asher called in Officer Chanel to escort Laurel to a different room, where she would explain the steps that would be taken to help her overcome the grief.

* * *

Days, and then weeks went by. The recovery process was grueling for everyone involved, but no one suffered more than Mark and Laurel. Mark saw his therapist on a daily basis where he was counseled, and his emotional status analyzed. It was also suggested that Laurel seek counseling to help her overcome the recent events. Trevor continued to stay active in Mark's life, being a big brother to him and guiding him in whatever way possible. The occasional outings Trevor took with Mark, such as to sports games and events helped Mark greatly. Mark was able to free his mind during these times and actually be a kid again.

One night, Trevor was going to sleep after a long day of work. As he rested his head, he almost immediately fell asleep and entered a lucid dream state. In this dream, Trevor was on the street corner in his neighborhood, about to walk up to his doorstep. The atmosphere was lovely, and the sun was in all its glory. The sky's beauty was indescribable, the purest blue and the clouds perfectly white. The depth and softness of the clouds were magnificent; one could almost feel it just with their eyes. As Trevor approached his house, he saw a man in all white sitting down on the front steps. Curious as to who this may be, he hastened his approach. The man was facing the opposite direction as if he was waiting for someone. As Trevor neared the man, he turned around, and it was Richard. The dream felt so real as if it was reality.

"Richard! Is this a dream again?" said Trevor as he hugged his best friend warmly.

Richard smiled before moving closer. "Yes, if you want to call it a dream, but it is more than that. I could have moved onto the other side for good long ago, but I asked the gatekeepers to let me stay on this plane until you found the answers you sought. Once you move onto the other side, you remain there forever, and the cares of this world will be no more. Even now, where I am, you see the peace can't be comprehended. Beyond the gates is a feeling I can't describe."

Trevor looked on with tears, but no longer with tears of grief, but rather, tears of solace.

Looking about, Richard continued to relish the beauty. "Just standing at the foot of it, one can feel immense peace. Serene couldn't wait to go beyond the gate, it was so beautiful. Everything outside of it, is a thing of the past; so, I am sure my wife has forgotten about me by now," Richard said in fun. "It is time I reconnect with her. The gatekeepers— some call them angels— explained to me what happened that night. Tell my son that I am not angry with him. When I think about it, I know it could have turned out much worse. I am just glad he was not hurt that day. Tell him that I want him to grow up to do better than I did. Tell him his father is at peace and that I want the same for him. I made a promise to the gatekeepers that after you found the answers you sought; I would move on. Now I must keep my word."

The whole time Richard talked, Trevor sat and listened, crying and overcome with emotion. He knew this would truly be the last time he would see his best friend.

"Thanks for everything Richard. Rest in peace," said Trevor filled with great sorrow, yet at the same time joy.

A great white light appeared at the end of the street as two figures of great stature stood illuminated.

"It is time Trevor. One day you and I will see each other again beyond the gates; but until then, live the life you're in to the fullest. Let nothing keep you down. Farewell Trevor."

Richard stood as he prepared to walk toward the great light that awaited him. Looking on, Trevor watched Richard as he approached the light, taking his time and relishing what was to come. As he finally approached the gate, one of the gatekeepers placed a hand upon Richard's shoulder as they walked slowly into the light. The three walked through the light until the greater light within the gates overtook them until they could be seen no more. The light slowly faded away as if it was never there. Trevor sat on his steps as the wind calmly blew and the trees gently swayed, accepting the fact that his friend was now truly gone. He was consoled by the fact that one day, years to come, the two would see each other once again.

Chapter 12

Life and Lemons, What Is Made of It

T revor woke to the sound of his wife making breakfast downstairs as he sat on the edge of his bed, mentally taking in the spiritual experiencing, knowing officially, Richard his best friend, has moved on.

"Honey! Breakfast is ready," Nadine called out.

"I'll be right down, one minute," Trevor answered as he continued to sit at the foot of the bed. Trevor considered what Richard told him in the vision, his words of encouragement, and most of all, his desire for Trevor to let Mark know, that everything was and will be alright. *Rest in peace friend.* Trevor stood to his feet before making his way downstairs to meet his wife.

Nadine sipped her coffee. "What's the matter? Are you alright?" She asked as he appeared more joyful than usual.

"Yes... yes, I'm okay. I was just mentally preparing myself for today's work, that's all," replied Trevor.

As he sat and enjoyed his breakfast, he suddenly imagined something spectacular he could do in Richard and Serene's names so that their deaths would not be in vain. Trevor hastily gulped down his breakfast, eager to tell the crew at the station.

"Slow down, sweetie, no need to be in a rush; you still have time to prepare," said Nadine as he devoured his food.

His cheeks puffed as they became filled. "I know, but there is something I have to relay to my colleagues as soon as possible. I'm going to go in early today."

Trevor finished his breakfast, hurried upstairs to freshen up, and returned downstairs to leave for work.

"Thanks for the great breakfast, honey. It was delicious, as usual. See you when I get back," He said this before kissing his wife on the forehead and heading off to work.

Trevor drove excitedly but carefully down the road in anticipation of sharing his idea. He knew deep down inside this would benefit many others and prevent future tragedies such as the one that took place with Richard and Serene.

When he got to the station, everyone couldn't help but notice how happy Trevor was, which was a welcome change since Richard's death.

"You look jolly today, Trevor. Won the lottery?" asked Chanel playfully.

Trevor nodded as he guffawed. "No, but I believe I came up with something even better. Do you know where Sheriff Asher is?"

"He's in his office," replied Chanel.

Trevor made his way down the hall and approached the sheriff. "Good morning, Asher. I have been thinking. What if somehow, I give a speech before a committee on the importance of gun safety and additional training for officers? No one was more knowledgeable than Richard when it came to this. But as we've seen, even the most experienced person can make just one mistake, that could lead to a tragedy. I believe speaking before a committee in the town of Welder Ville about the importance of proper gun storage will help to prevent future occurrences of gun accidents."

Sheriff Asher listened attentively, appearing optimistic. "I couldn't have thought of a better idea myself. Let's get started with the plan right away; we can start by contacting local news and other organizations. I'm sure we will get fast responses. This could save hundreds of lives in the long run. I'm sure Richard would be proud of this decision."

Asher and Trevor let Chanel in on the idea before gathering others, all in hopes of bringing the plan to fruition.

Over the next few days, aside from doing their usual criminal investigations and research, the unit was hard at work reaching out to local news teams and board committees. The Welder Ville police unit was well known for their outstanding service in their community, so it was just a matter of time before they began receiving replies. After days of reaching out to different news teams, many agreed to cover the talk and a number of committees reached out to the unit about how they could help the cause.

"Man, I never expected so many would be ready to support us on such short notice. Wow, I couldn't be any more grateful," said Trevor.

No one could disagree with this statement. Everyone was surprised at the outpouring of love from the community.

"Tell me about it. It's like the people who contact us demand we let them help in any way possible. I guess people were moved by such a respectable person like Richard. Combine that with Mark, who innocently caused such a tragedy, and you have created a situation where many feel compelled to help. Are you prepared to speak on July 10th? The news media and many people will have their eyes glued to you. I just want you to be ready," Chanel said with concern.

Trevor, as always, considered Chanel's point of view, but in this instance, he wholeheartedly disagreed.

"Chanel, what I plan to say on July 10th is from my heart and soul. I have no need to practice something that is being spoken from within. Teaching and helping save others is a necessity for me. If it were up to me, I would give the talk today without a second thought," said Trevor passionately.

Everyone saw that Trevor was ready to give this speech and they could not wait to hear the wisdom he would relay to the public.

Chanel smiled. She trusted Trevor. But she still liked the idea of preparing. "Okay, but we must practice and get the speech down on paper, or at least some of it. I say let's get started writing it now."

Trevor's thoughts went from mind to paper; they flowed effortlessly. Chanel was there to help type it out and give it a little fine tuning; she even offered helpful input on what should be added. Over the span of a few days, on their lunch breaks, the two took the time to compile the speech. In the end, the hard work and time paid off.

"And I think we're done," Chanel said. "Great job, Trevor. Your words are sure to resonate with everyone who hears them. You're doing a great service. Asher already said you can take a half day, so it's time you get going and rest before tomorrow. You know, you must look good for the cameras; this is going to be a big event. Lots of news stations will come to see the Welder Ville unit. I am sure you will make us, and the town, look outstanding."

Trevor absorbed the words of encouragement. "Thanks, Chanel."

Trevor went home for the day to rest and prepare for the big speech tomorrow. He was nervous but confident that his words would inspire and elevate the listeners.

In the morning, Nadine was just as, if not more, nervous as Trevor.

"I know you're well-prepared hon. You look confident and ready to go. The children and I will watch you on television. It's so nice you're not only doing this to save lives, but for Richard and Serene also. I know he would have wanted you and everyone to make the best out of such a terrible situation, and you're going above and beyond to do just that," she said as they sat down for breakfast.

Trevor sat down at the table and embraced his children in a big huddle; enjoying the uplifting feeling he got from their very presence. Trevor looked his wife and each of his children passionately in the eyes. "If it weren't for you guys, none of this would be possible. You guys inspire me to get up every morning and be the best I can be. You guys inspire me to accomplish what seems impossible, so I just want to say thank you, and most importantly, I love you all."

"Daddy, will we see you on television today?" asked one of his children.

Of all the people he was nervous about seeing him speak, none made him more nervous than his children. He wanted to be the best he could be before them.

"Yes, Daddy will be on television today giving a very important talk. You, your mommy, your brother and sister will all be watching me. When I get back, I want you all to tell me if I did well or not." Trevor was so caught up in the moment that he was almost late. "You guys finish up your breakfast and help out Mommy while I get ready." Trevor left his family to their meal. He knew that day would be a monumental one. When he came downstairs dressed, and ready to go, his face was full of glee and excitement. Trevor grabbed his jacket. "It's time I get going. Don't forget to tune in. I will need your constructive criticism when I return."

His children and his wife looked at him with pride and joy. "You're going to do very well up there. Now, get going before you're late," said his wife.

As Trevor drove down the road, he hoped that his speech would touch the lives of many. He hoped many would take heed of his words of wisdom, as well as hoping to inspire people for years to come. He imagined how it would play out; a confident man standing boldly before many without fear. The only fear in his mind at that moment was the fear that his words would not reach enough people. Most of all, he was doing this for Mark. He hoped that when Mark looked back on this speech in the years to come, he would know everything was okay, that he should have no regrets but always seek to inspire and help others.

After a long and thoughtful drive, Trevor pulled up to the back entrance of headquarters to avoid the press upfront. He stopped his car and looked at all the press and news media from a distance.

"I guess this is it, no going back now," Trevor said to himself. He entered the station through a back door, where many of his co-workers were waiting for him. Asher, Maribel, and Chanel greeted him as he entered.

"You look ready Trevor and man, your suit, it looks sharp," Officer Chanel said flashing a smile. "One of the people in charge of setting up the event is waiting for you up ahead. Whenever you're ready to go, you can just let him know that you're set."

"Looking good," Sheriff Asher responded. "Go out there and make everyone proud."

Maribel smiled proudly at Trevor. "They are waiting for you. Go out there and let your wisdom resonate."

Trevor let one of the men in charge of the event know that he was ready. He was escorted to the door and as he walked towards the exit, he saw the podium and thousands of faces ready to hear him speak. Trevor tried not to let his anxiety get in the way of spreading a message he knew would impact many lives in the future.

"You're set to go. Good luck," said the escort.

Trevor stepped outside the station where he walked towards the podium. Cameras clicked and flashed, and people stared with anticipation. He quickly composed himself and began the speech.

"Good afternoon, ladies and gentlemen, children, boys, and girls. Yes, I mention all these categories because this speech is for each and every one of you, born and unborn. Recently, as many know, we lost someone dear to our town and our community, Richard. To describe him in words is difficult. To truly understand the characteristics he possessed, one would have to have known him personally. Some words I can use to describe him are humble, conscientious, disciplined, reliable, generous, teacher; the list just goes on and on, and any who were blessed to have met him would understand this. As for his wife Serene, who unfortunately lost her life the same night. It was because of her that Richard possessed many of these qualities. She inspired Richard to be the best father and husband any man could wish to be; he became greater each day just to inspire those around him and make them proud. Serene was a mother and sister to all who were in her company; she never saw anyone who happened to know her as friends, but rather family. For those of you who may not know, Richard and Serene lost their lives in one of the most unfortunate ways imaginable. The reason it happened is why I am giving this speech. Mark, dear Mark, the young son of Richard and Serene, in an act of innocence and good intentions mistakenly took their lives. In short, Richard, who was always careful and strict about gun safety, happened to forget, just one time to properly store his weapon. Richard placed his jacket on his table and inside the jacket was his service pistol. Mark awoke early in the morning, saw his dad's coat on the table, and when he inspected it, he spotted his dad's firearm.

"Richard taught his son about gun safety at a very young age, just as his father did with him, so Mark knew of the danger. Mark proceeded to pick up the gun and carry it upstairs to give to his father, so that it may be properly stored. Richard was in a deep sleep and didn't register Mark's efforts to wake him. Unfortunately, Mark was shaking Richard with the same hand that grasped the firearm. Eventually, the weapon discharged, and the bullet pierced both Serene and Richard, which resulted in their passing. Mark had only good intentions in keeping his family safe and unfortunately, it had the opposite result.

"Today, I propose to you all 'Mark's Law,' named in honor of Mark for trying to do what is right. Under Mark's Law, all officers and even regular citizens who possess registered firearms must receive further training in proper gun safety. Mark's Law will also branch out into schools, reaching grades as early as first, and recommending that children should be home-schooled about this as early as age six. The goal of Mark's Law is to hopefully put an end to accidental killings. Of course, accidents are just that, accidents. Therefore, some individuals may still forget to properly store their weapons, but with Mark's Law in place, it will help to greatly reduce these mistakes. I knew Richard basically my whole life, and he would want us to take this tragedy and turn it into something positive, so now I am doing just that.

"Starting next month, I plan to execute Mark's Law with the help of politicians. All neighboring schools are to begin adding the material to their curriculum. Just teaching about this one day of every month should be enough to embed it in the minds of our youth and even those teaching it. Once a student is introduced to Mark's Law in school, or at home, hopefully, that individual will relay what he was taught to friends and family all over. This information is not meant to only be local, but my hope is that it spreads as far and wide as possible. It was an honor and pleasure to speak with you all today and share this information. I cannot do this alone, but with your cooperation, this will surely be a success. Thank you all and God bless."

Trevor's speech would forever stick with those who heard it; everyone was beyond proud. He stayed a while longer to answer any questions journalists had. Judging by everyone's reaction, they seemed ready to implement "Mark's Law" with full faith that it will help to end such terrible tragedies. After a few more minutes of questions and answers, the meeting was concluded. Trevor was confident that it went better than expected and knew that he had sown a seed of positive change.

An hour after his talk, everyone in attendance had already left the vicinity. Trevor headed back into the building to see his coworkers. Everyone gathered, as they applauded and congratulated him on such a monumental moment. Trevor was overwhelmed with gratitude and a sense of accomplishment. He was able to see the appreciation that they had for his speech; as well as being pleased that his vision already, touched the lives of many.

"Thank you guys, thank you, this means so much to me, thank you," said Trevor as they continued to clap and congratulate him. All Trevor could do then was smile and soak in the applause, which everyone was intent on him receiving. After the applause finally stopped, Trevor provided a few more words to his coworkers. "This was only possible with your help. Your words of encouragement during our hard times helped to motivate me. Your words to keep pushing forward and let go of the pain and sorrow helped me to envision greatness. So again, I just want to thank you all."

At once, his co-workers surrounded him to provide warm hugs, while some gave him friendly nudges. He laughed and enjoyed the moment, knowing brighter and better days were ahead.

Those at Aunt Laurel's home finished watching Trevor's speech on television. She was filled with emotion as she cried tears of joy hearing Trevor talk about Richard, Serene, and Mark. The passion with which he spoke for Mark and the fact that he even dedicated a law in his name was truly monumental. Laurel was aware that Mark couldn't possibly understand how much his law would change the world at that moment, but in the future, he would grasp it and hopefully, even help uphold that which was created in his name.

Laurel embraced Mark. He was watching and realized Trevor was on television, but he was not fully able to comprehend his friend's purpose up there. One thing he did pick up on was when Trevor mentioned "Mark's Law," a law dedicated to him.

"Aunt Laurel, what is Mark's Law?" Mark asked curiously.

Laurel looked at him with glee and found it difficult to give him an answer, but she summoned the best one she could think of at the moment. "Mark's Law is a law dedicated to a very special young boy, a boy that your dad was very proud of. In years to come, you will understand more and appreciate it."

Mark gave her an inquisitive look for a few moments before continuing to look at the television. They had made so much emotional progress since the passing of Richard and Serene, and this moment would surely help lead to the complete healing of them both.

Bertha, like Laurel and many others, was moved to tears of joy and appreciation. Haden had left the house after realizing she was watching Trevor speak on television. After what happened, he never wanted to see Trevor's face again. Bertha enjoyed this moment of accomplishment alone and in pure joy. She hadn't felt so proud and joyful in years, especially since the passing of her brother. Richard and Serene were very special to Bertha and to know that their names were being honored, it moved her dearly. Even in death, she knew Richard would continue to help save lives, as he would have if he were still there.

"I love you Richard, I love you, Serene. You two will always be a beacon of affection and love. Thanks for everything," Bertha said to herself with deep gratitude.

The signs of growth concerning "Mark's Law" were slow but apparent. A few weeks after Trevor's talk, he was invited to speak at many schools. Trevor had yet to reject one offer. No matter the distance and time it took out of his day, Trevor made it his duty to fulfill each and every request. With each visit, he gave motivation and hope. He detailed how Mark's Law was already helping to impact lives in many ways. The students were engaged; they actively participated in the talks by asking questions and giving suggestions about how they could contribute to the cause. Parents made it their duty to implement Mark's Law within parent-teacher organizations, to make sure it was a part of the school. Trevor couldn't have wished for a better outcome. Weeks turned to months; months turned to years and the success of Mark's Law caught everyone off guard.

Nine years later, the success of Mark's Law in Welder Ville and nearby towns was so great that other towns and cities utilized it themselves. Many small programs opened solely for this purpose, and the methods had greatly improved with the help of the community. Many teachers and parents had personally written to Trevor concerning their young ones. These letters detailed how their children have grown in other ways under the guidance of Mark's Law, becoming young men and women who are inspired to be protectors of society. Parents also realized that they had escaped many potentially devastating outcomes by gaining awareness of Mark's Law. Trevor was not proud of himself or the program; Trevor was instead proud of the people who grew because of it and sought to make their neighborhoods and homes safer places utilizing what they learned.

Chapter 13
The War Was Necessary

O ver the nine years that had passed, much had changed at the Welder Ville Detective Unit. Trevor was now Sheriff, and it was his turn to lead, guide, and mold future standup citizens as himself. Even more, he was the first black Sheriff of the town, which made the moment even more special. Asher was retired, but Trevor was aware that he never would have become the person he was without Asher's help and guidance. Asher was always there for him since Trevor's early years at the station, guiding and pushing him to be the best he could be on a daily basis.

Trevor's children had matured greatly and were in high school. His wife seemed to have not aged in anything but wisdom and kindness. The fruits Trevor had produced were fruits of kindness, leadership, joy, and happiness. Trevor had no regrets or sorrows in his life; he knew everything that happened, happened for a reason. Through all those reasons, he saw the beauty that came out of them.

Officer Chanel was married, and she too had left the Welder Ville Detective Unit. Chanel could never have wished for a better job in the world. She never regretted her time spent there. She, on the other hand, felt it was her duty to dedicate her time to her newborn daughter

Damaris as a stay-at-home mom. The unit was like her second home, and therefore she still visited from time to time and everyone appreciated her appearances, whenever they may have been.

Corporal Maribel became chief deputy. Even though she was sad to see some faces leave the unit, she was beyond proud to see the growth that had taken place. With Trevor as sheriff, she knew the unit was still in good hands and growth was sure to continue. She was proud of the many new faces that had arrived and knew they would be molded to be the best they could be with the help of the whole team. Maribel saw herself remaining with the unit for many more years to come.

Bertha had made great strides over the years, but her best decision was letting go of Haden. She was proud and grateful to have experienced the love of her brother Richard. If not for him, she would not have realized that love was never present in her ex-husband Haden. It took a little time for her to realize this, but it was better late than never. She happily remarried, finding someone she never imagined would come into her life, who showed her the love she always wanted, and more. Bertha visited her brother and Serene's graves from time to time, to witness true love. A love so great and true that even death could not part them. Bertha believed in her heart that Richard asked God in heaven to send her such a husband on his behalf, for she believed he could have not come into her life any other way.

Mark displayed tremendous development. Everyone saw an almost surreal change in him. Now fifteen years old, Mark was always special in the eyes of everyone who knew him, but soon he was displaying peculiar traits. Peculiar in the sense that he endured such a tragedy at a young age, but he used it to help himself excel, while at the same time, changing the lives of others. Teaching them to use their mistakes to create something positive. Mark wanted to follow in his father's footsteps to become an officer and detective. He eventually would join the youth academy which trained young adults in becoming standup officers.

Mark thought about his father daily and he truly missed him every day. He would come to understand Mark's Law and its purpose. He knew he had a duty to uphold and spread it as much as possible; he didn't see this as a job or burden but rather, he took pride and joy in doing so. Mark no longer needed therapy to cope with the tragic event; he had come to grips with what happened. He had forgiven himself just as his father Richard wanted. Mark continued to meditate on all the things his father said to him as a kid such as, "you're amazing," "you will grow up to be special," "you will be greater than I am" and "you make me proud." Mark knew Richard was living through the things he instilled in him as a kid, and Mark's goal was to apply those words to his life every day.

* * *

Back at the unit, Trevor arrived at work. Every day he made it his duty to look up at a list of names of people who came before him. He looked at two names in particular, Richard and Asher. Two men who helped him to get where he wanted and beyond. Trevor made this a habit over the years without missing a day.

"Good morning there, Sheriff, looking better than ever this morning. You know, it's been a while since I said this, and I just want to say it again. You have made Welder Ville more beautiful than it ever was.

You made this unit grow in ways no one would have imagined, changing all who have been in your presence. I just want to say thanks for all your service and hard work Trevor," said Chief Maribel.

Trevor was humbled by the speech. "Thanks, Maribel. But the true thanks go to all who came before me, like Asher, who helped me to become who I am today. If I do things better than those who came before me, it is only because they pushed me to do better and now, I do the same for others. Seeing such a strong and charismatic woman like you every day held me up during my hard times. Watching the officers come to work every day, makes me reflect on where I started. When I see them, I see the younger me, and it brightens my day to see the great potential in them all. I thank everyone collectively for their presence," replied Trevor.

Maribel gave a smile of appreciation in response to his unfailing encouragement.

Trevor went into his office where he unpacked his bag as he sat in his chair. Trevor paused to look at a picture of him and Richard on his desk. Leaning back, he folded his hands and looked about his office with a smile, knowing this was all possible through Richard's wisdom in life, and in death.

After Richard's death, the unit operated on a physical and spiritual level, being an inspiration to many. With a strong leader such as Trevor in place, Asher didn't have to worry about the department. Welder Ville continued to grow, and its presence is forever appreciated by all in the community, and beyond.